THE ASHE WALKER CHRONICLES

Saga #2: And the Faces of Resilience

Abbix Publishing Company

Contents

1

THE LIGHT SHINES

"That's a little much," Ashe's father, Dan, said with surprise and admiration. "Even for you, son." Dan's face was almost expressionless, but his eyes betrayed his pride as he looked at his son.

"We're treating them well, though." Ashe looked his father in the eye, keeping his face stoic. "I promise. We only have so much to give without taking in three extra people, but the new farmers are doing their best."

"I know that," Dan reassured. "What's making me nervous is you. You're going in too hot."

Ashe stopped for a moment to contemplate his decisions. The idea of starting a small vocational initiative in the worst part of the district—possibly the planet—so that society's lowest class could grow into a fighting force seemed, at the least, illogical.

It was too early to take in three hostages, and Ashe knew it. However, his dream and their ambitions for a better world had blinded him. The Outcasts had no money, no resources, no experience, and, most importantly, no fighting skills. Ashe's initiative had given some of the Outcasts basic skills like farming and plumbing, but most of these teachings hadn't been applied. Only farming had begun, and it was still in its early phases and far from a productive experience to build upon. So, Ashe's guilt stirred again, and the three hostages started to look like a mistake.

"I've thought about it before," Ashe confessed with a lowered gaze, "and I don't think I can go back."

"You're right." Dan smiled with a nod. "You can't."

"What do I do?"

"You've grown, son," Dan said, with a tear sliding down his cheek. "I... I can't believe you're finally here."

"Here?" Ashe was confused for a moment. The Hollows wasn't in any parent's dreams for their child.

"Don't stop, Ashe," Dan said, looking him in the eye. Dan was choking up, and he pressed his lips together in a small smile.

Ashe, noticing his father's emotions, let a tear slip down his cheek.

"You're showing your emotions, too," Dan whispered with a hand on his mouth.

"I've... learned a lot," Ashe admitted with a smile. "Thank you for everything you've done for me and for what you did for Mom."

"You don't have to thank me," Dan reassured him. "Just don't let it go to waste."

"I promise I won't." Ashe nodded. The last time he had seen his father, Ashe had been angry and impulsive. He had complained constantly about the systems in place to keep them subjugated, but he had never dreamed that he would be making decisions that decided the futures of his peers.

"So, what are you going to do now?" Dan asked cheekily, a smile curling his lips.

Ashe stayed silent for a moment, looking at his father. Ashe knew the question was a test.

What am I going to do? Ashe's mind stopped and changed gears mid-conversation. *Is he implying I should return the hostages? He must know that's too risky. Those three are young, and they might report everything they learned while they were in the Hollows. Plus, getting them out of their hole is hard enough on its own. So, what am I going to do?*

"Attaboy, son!" Dan slapped Ashe on his back, bringing him back to reality.

Ashe's eyebrows knit into a puzzle. "I didn't say anything?"

"You stopped and thought about it!" Dan cheered.

Ashe burst out in a laugh. "I was that bad, wasn't I?" Ashe said, his laughter trailing off as he blushed.

Dan laughed. "You have no idea."

***

"Food distribution is good for now, but..." Hunter said, scratching his beard, "One of them is getting a little feisty."

"The blond one?" Ashe asked flatly.

Hunter nodded with a mix of disgust and boredom.

After a pause, which he spent formulating his words, Ashe said, "I was thinking about the whole situation with these three and everything going on, and I think we need to slow down."

"What do you mean?" Hunter crossed his arms and turned to fully face Ashe.

"The last week has been wild," Ashe said bluntly, looking at Hunter with a knowing look. "Since the day we caught them, security's been ransacking every building, and we can't move around the Hollows as freely as before. We didn't realize it back then, but we needed that cover of seeming weak and insignificant."

Hunter's eyes flared a little, although he didn't turn away. "If things go back to how they were before, then they don't show us as much attention as they do the other stratifications. We're too insignificant to be a part of their world to begin with. I know that's not true, but that's their biggest mistake."

Hunter raised an eyebrow at Ashe, intrigued by the idea. "That's... okay."

"Hiding is the best option we have right now until we get something of a foothold," Ashe said. "Remember, none of us know how to fight. It took five of us to sloppily take down three of their newer recruits who lacked the experience and skills of the older ranks. Ben and Sam, Harry's friends, were able to stand their ground against one of them despite their age. My experiences with the guards back home were a little different."

"Involving more blood, I assume," Hunter said jokingly, then his face straightened when Ashe's dead-serious gaze fell upon him.

"Much more," Ashe said.

"Sorry if I..." Hunter's eyes went to the ground in shame.

"Don't worry about it." Ashe's hand magically appeared on Hunter's shoulder, making Hunter jump in surprise.

"Where's Nolan?" Ashe said.

"Laying low for now," Hunter said, a smile sneaking onto his face. "I told him I'd cover your shift since you were with your dad, but here you are."

"Thanks, man." Ashe smiled.

"Seems like you had a good talk," Hunter teased.

"You noticed?"

As the two exchanged their looks, Ashe enjoyed Hunter's warming presence and longed to see Max and Caleb, who had been the same comfort and more to him before he'd become an Outcast. Hunter's cheeky positivity and unwavering determination that always burst forward made Ashe feel oddly at home.

"So, what now?" Hunter said after a pause.

"We're sending them back," Ashe said, his fingers wandering to his chin, a habit he'd developed since coming to the Hollows.

"Just like that?" Hunter said right away.

"They'll deliver a statement that says we're going away," Ashe said, "or going out of business or anything that implies we're going to stop doing what we're doing."

"That might entice them, though," Hunter said, deep in thought. "If we back off, it means we're afraid. If they as much as smell any hesitation, we're in trouble."

"Ball's in our court, huh?" Ashe said, looking at the ground with a slight laugh.

"What?"

"My dad told me that." Ashe looked up, remembering he was still with Hunter. "The ball's now in our court, and we have to decide quickly."

"What if we took them out of the city?" Hunter suggested suddenly. "They don't have to find out that those three were kidnapped. We've been hiding our faces from them, and they don't know where they are."

"That's right," Ashe said, realizing the biggest advantage they had was their anonymity. Ashe caught a glimpse of Hunter's train of thought. "They don't know we're actually against the system."

"We can take them outside the city and leave them a good distance out there for the rest of the forces to find," Hunter said, then his face changed color. "The problem is that boy Harry and his friends, though. They could be recognized since the guards saw them the night they were attacked."

"We have to keep them out of sight at all costs," Ashe said. "And I thought we finally got them out of this."

"They might not know full well what they've gotten themselves into," Hunter consoled him, knowing how much Ashe blamed himself for Harry and his friends starting this whole dilemma. "But regardless of what they thought, they have to deal with the consequences of their decision. They started this—partially, but still. You're trying too hard to protect them."

Ashe looked at Hunter silently, comparing the two voices in his head. Hunter's voice was telling him not to worry, but his mind blamed him for getting kids involved in the start of a revolution.

"What would Caleb do?" Ashe said suddenly, with eyes devoid of expression.

"Caleb?"

"A friend I knew before the crowning," Ashe said. "He was raised Professional, and he's really smart. Whenever we got into trouble or needed to get something done, and he started to think, he would get this look on his face. We nicknamed it the calculator face."

"What kind of person was he?"

"Smart sums it up, pretty much." Ashe smiled reminiscently. "He wasn't as feisty as I was, but he did have his problems with the government and all."

"I would expect *that*," Hunter said.

"Yeah. Now, let's consider our possible options," Ashe said.

"First option, we put them out in the middle of nowhere, or at least as far from here as possible, for their friends to pick them up," Hunter said. "This is, theoretically, the safer option. We wait for things to cool down, and we keep doing what we are doing."

"Since keeping them here is out of the question, our second option is to make our guests an offer," Ashe said, maintaining as calm a gaze as he could.

Hunter raised an eyebrow and clenched his jaw.

"Tell me you're not thinking what I think you are," Hunter said, almost pleading. "Have you finally lost your mind?"

"We have pretty much nothing to offer," Ashe nodded, "but they don't have to know that. All we need is information."

"Okay," Hunter said, sighing with relief.

"Asking them to join comes later down the line." Ashe winked as his hand magically poked Hunter's shoulder again, making him take a step back.

"Man!" Hunter exclaimed.

Ashe laughed. "Who's doing the negotiations?"

Ashe's face became serious, and he turned to the stairs of the school building, wondering again how the stairs were still intact.

"I'll back you up." Hunter patted him on the back gently.

Ashe, throughout his Worker upbringing, hadn't been much of a people person. His rebellious nature had won him friends, but he always seemed to keep his distance from other people and focus on his own life. Yet, the speeches he'd given in front of the Hollows' school had brought something out of Ashe he never knew was there: the strength to attract people and drive them. He knew he was good at giving people the extra push they needed. His fiery nature set his charismatic presence alight, and his passion elevated him when he spoke to people. His confidence in the spotlight gradually grew speech by speech, and he became naturally acquainted with the crowd, especially those who shared his dreams.

Max would laugh at this, wouldn't he? Ashe caught himself thinking as he went up the stairs. When they reached the second floor, the blindfolded guards, sitting on the floor in a circle, came into view.

"What do you want?" a disgusted voice snarled at Ashe and Hunter's presence.

"To talk," Ashe said calmly, looking at the guard's blindfolded face.

"Our suits record—"

"We destroyed all the filming equipment and listening devices," Hunter said bluntly, barely hiding the pleasure he felt.

"You're good for people who only have some dirt for food," the guard said, his disgusted voice keeping its edge.

Ashe's jaw clicked as he ground his teeth, and he immediately found Hunter's hand on his chest.

"Wait," Hunter mouthed to Ashe.

"We're letting you go," Hunter said after a long pause, his words breaking the silence.

"What?"

"We're letting you go once we have our talk," Ashe said.

"What's the catch? Where's the trap?" the disgusted guard asked reluctantly.

"Tell us about your training."

2

A New Home

Max dropped onto his bed heavily, his bones aching from the day's work. His duties had evolved from the first and second floors to include the third and fourth, and a joint responsibility for the chimney with Nate, who didn't look close to tiring out. Max had grown tired of listening, and his skin battled with the harsh chemicals.

As he lay on his bed and stared at the ceiling, Max's analytical engine turned off and took a break, letting exhaustion take over him. His muscles, which had grown since he'd become a Servant, dragged his body down with their soreness. To his own surprise, Max's mind didn't think, and no train of thought powered through his head. A silent void, where breath came with effort, reigned dominant over his mind and his body. As he lay there, his body weighed down by exhaustion, his mind sank into mental fatigue. His thoughts, once vibrant and agile, now struggled to form coherent patterns. The relentless demands and harsh treatment he'd faced had taken their toll, eroding his spirit day by day.

Max's inner fight was still alive, although it had weakened from a roaring flame to a spark. A fog settled on his dreams and memories, making him long to sink into the comfort of the past. Memories of Ashe slowly faded out of his head, only kept alive by Max's will and desire for a reunion. Max yearned for solace, for a respite in his friend's presence from the ceaseless demands consuming his every waking moment. He longed for a flicker of hope to guide him out of the darkness that trapped him. But, for the moment, all he could do was lie where he did, giving his body what rest he was allowed for it to work properly again.

"Somebody's looking down," Nate's voice broke the overbearing silence.

"Hey." Max looked up at Nate, whose clothes were covered in black smoke and his beard caked in dirt. Max sat up just enough to be looking straight at Nate. "What happened?"

"The usual," Nate said casually as he went to the closet doors.

"If you've got another story, it'd really help," Max said. "Things are getting dark here."

"Six months is a long time, I have to say," Nate said. "You've been holding out well since you got the last promotion. When was that, anyways?"

"Like three months ago," Max said, looking through his memories. "I don't really care."

"How do you think Ashe's doing?" Nate said warmly, a hint of compassion in his voice.

Since Max's last promotion, the time he spent with Nate gave him solace in the midst of all the chaos around him. The time they spent in the mansion's chimney, isolated from the rest of the world, felt to Max like a trip. They went inside his mind with his memories and thoughts playing out on the pitch-black walls around them, with Nate as his trusty companion.

"He hasn't shown up," Max said. "Ideally, he might have started looking for me and Caleb. That doesn't sound real, though."

"You're getting somewhere," Nate affirmed. "You know what? I'll tell you another story. Remember the same fool Professional kid with the fiancé who drew Servant?"

"He's etched into my head by now," Max said, leaning back and closing his eyes for a listening session.

"Great," Nate said as he got out of the closet, now dressed in his sleep clothes, a simple shirt, and pants, just enough to protect him from the cold. "After his first year of initiation, the little kid came to terms with the fact that his life had been altered, and like you, he started listening. It was the only activity he had, after all. So, the days turned into weeks, the weeks turned into months, and the months turned into seasons. Every season or two, the boy's duty would jump around between floors, and the mansion's owner liked his competence.

"So, the boy's treatment got a little better, a little more food, better clothes, and he started feeling some relief. The golden days of privilege weren't all gone just yet, he thought. And he cruised along, enjoying his special treatment, until a new Servant arrived.

"The girl was, to the boy's surprise, Servant-raised. Kind, obedient, and just as good-looking as the boy. Then, the quarters were split in two. One for him and one for the new girl, and none was allowed to step into the other's quarters or even see the other's quarters. For her initiation, the girl took the first floor, as the boy had, and she stayed out of his sight for a good two months. Then, suddenly, the girl took his place on the third floor, and he was dropped to the first and second."

"Jealousy?" Max cut in.

"Don't get ahead of yourself," Nate teased. "This one's long, I know. The good part is coming."

"Honestly, this kid sounds like another miserable fool who believed in the system," Max said, a little more forcefully than he intended. "I would say he should have known, but…"

"You're right," Nate said, sniffling. Max looked up to see a teary-eyed Nate staring at his soul. "He should have."

Guilt devoured Max immediately. *I was being rude,* Max thought.

"Sorry," Max said, sitting straight up. "I didn't mean to be impatient."

"Don't worry about it," Nate said with a reassuring smile. "Long story short, the boy was outperformed, and he fell back into his hole. But the girl wasn't evil. She just did her job a little better than he did, and slowly, he felt more and more cornered by his fate."

"I kinda get it," Max smiled as he spoke.

"What do you get?" Nate said quietly.

"Where he went wrong," Max said. "You want to say it was his fault, right?"

Nate nodded, waiting for more.

"He relied too much on what was given to him."

"Uh-huh," Nate followed with his right index finger propped under his chin. The brief burst of sadness that appeared a few minutes before had disappeared, leaving a more focused, barely blinking face staring at Max.

"He didn't try doing anything on his own..." Max started as if testing his own conclusions. "Right?"

"Yep." Nate nodded a few times in succession, his head swinging in harmony with his speech. "His delusions of being special made him think that he'd only have to show everyone how great he was in order to get the appreciation he deserved."

"So, the point is to go the extra mile, sort of, right?" Max said.

"Exactly," Nate said slowly.

"What comes after listening?" Max said with a humble face and wide eyes.

Max, despite his misery and exhaustion, appreciated Nate telling him the story. Nate wasn't talkative nor sociable, yet he always provided Max with the peace he needed without asking for anything back.

"Anna and company are talking," Nate said, laying back on his bed. "They've grown tired, you can say. That's a place to start."

"Sounds promising."

"Aim big," Nate said, looking up at the ceiling. "Or high, I don't know."

"Do you really think I can do something?" Max couldn't help himself from asking. Nate's constant willingness to help made Max feel even more guilty.

"Well, what do you know right now?" Nate said. "From listening and all."

"His business is booming, so to say," Max said rather formally. "Deals are going on everywhere and with everyone."

"But?" Nate said, reading between Max's words.

"He's as unhappy as we see," Max said with disgust. "Edward Junior and Sarah are still traveling. It's been two months now. I don't know if that's affecting him too much, though. He thinks more about us than about them."

"How old are they, anyways?" Nate said scornfully.

"Edward's twenty-five, and Sarah's twenty-one," Max said. "Their trip has something to do with her turning twenty-one. University or something like that. They're not part of the picture here, so we don't need to care that much, I suppose. He is worried about an upcoming deal, though. Even his wife's getting some of the... temper."

"How worried?" Nate said.

"Enough to go from room to room on his phone talking about it and managing every detail," Max said, surprised that Nate was asking follow-up questions. "It's nothing too exciting. Do you have any news?"

"Like I said, Anna and company are getting tired. Anna especially," Nate said.

"She seems like the brightest, though," Max's thoughts blurted through his mouth. "I always wonder why she's as committed as she is."

"Edna's brewing something," Nate said, his tone changing drastically. A dark shroud fell upon his words, taking them into a terrain he knew Max would want to explore.

"Brewing?" Max said, knowing Nate expected it.

"The nurse is at the center of the action right now," Nate said, his voice ebbing and flowing with its new dark tone, maintaining Max's complete attention. "His heart is already beat up pretty bad. She's trying to slow it down just enough."

Max sat up immediately, worry on his face, but Nate continued talking, forcing him to wait.

"Edna's had enough. Anna's had enough. You see where this is going, right?"

"Slowing it down is not the right thing to do," Max stated.

"What other option do they have?" Nate said.

"Murder is not the right thing to do," Max stated. "Spilling blood doesn't solve anything."

"Even you have to admit it's the only solution for some things," Nate challenged.

"It's too early for that, though," Max said. "There are other solutions now. Flight is the best one, in my opinion."

As Max's mind started working and analyzing again, images of Thorn screaming in the solitude of his huge mansion flashed wildly in his head. He had sometimes dreamt of getting rid of Thorn one way or another, but he had never considered the aftermath.

The thought of a free life no longer existed. Max even caught himself too many times wondering what a free life really was. Ashe and Caleb might have an idea, and that itself made Max feel free. He drew his strength from others around him. As Max analyzed the situation and his conclusions started forming, he thought about Anna, Edna, and the nurse's feelings with his analytical engine's colorless calculations. Yet, a flame of hope ignited somewhere inside him. The flame was distant, weak, and fading.

"Do you think we could?" Max said after a long pause, not sure if Nate was still awake.

"We could what?" Nate teased, smiling as he lay on his back.

"Run away," Max struggled to form the words as if the quarters' oppressing essence stopped him.

"I already told you," Nate said. "You're special, Max."

Max's mind finished its calculations, and his heart drew its fantasies, and he came upon an image of a vast wilderness, spreading as far as his eyes could see. The sun was low on the horizon, and the air was silent, cooled by the winter's night closing in. Max faced the wilderness with an open heart and a clear mind. As Max's mind worked, a smile appeared on his face.

Can I really? Max started wondering. *Will I really?*

"Someone's in a good mood," Nate said happily. "Don't lose that smile, kid."

"Are you helping them?" Max said, realizing he had delayed his mind's questions.

"Here and there," Nate admitted. "Not nearly enough, though. They are doing most of the work right now. They might need us later on."

"Us?" Max said, happiness now clearly audible in his voice.

"I'll tell Anna," Nate said.

"Tell the boy from your stories he doesn't need to give up," Max said suddenly.

"Give up?"

"Tell him he's still alive," Max said. "He doesn't have to stop because of an old mistake. There's always hope, and he knows that, but I think he doesn't want to admit it. Tell him his life is going to start again."

3

ECHOES OF REMORSE

"**Y**ou okay?" Caleb said, closing the door as Dave jumped into the dorm room.

"Yeah, I don't think anyone saw me," Dave said, struggling to catch his breath.

"What's new?" Eric said, looking away from the computer on his desk.

"Preparations for the new year, pretty much," Dave said, sitting down. "Some stuff regarding the new semester and the power distribution for an extension to the campus. It's going to be a whole new building."

"Nothing much, eh?" Eric tsked. "The semester is nearly over, and we don't have any big leads."

"The first one is enough, in my opinion," Caleb stated. "Too bad we can't play around with anything."

"You already saw what they've been doing since they found out somebody was just looking at their logs," Dave said. "Security is already tight enough around here. What do you think they'd do if they found out somebody was trying to edit anything?"

"And we don't even know how to deal with the system yet." Eric huffed, tapping his foot on the ground impatiently.

"What else can we do?" Caleb said as he leaned on the wall by Eric's wardrobe.

"Focus on passing the finals if we're being smart about this," Dave said after a pause.

"Do you think if we stick around, we might learn something here that could help us?" Caleb said, moving away from the wall and swinging a finger in the air in a perfect circle near his chin as he voiced his thoughts.

"That..." Eric started, then he stopped, allowing his mind to compute what he heard.

"That's smart, actually," Dave said. "Using the knowledge they gave us against them."

"We're too impatient for that, though," Eric said bluntly. "We must do something big before the year ends."

"Let history know that this year's Crowning was special," Caleb said.

"Crowning..." Eric thought out loud as his chin fell into his palm. His leg stopped moving.

"You got something?" Dave said, noticing Eric's awkward stillness.

"We weren't Crowned alone, right?" Eric said, looking up at the other two.

The two nodded in unison.

Eric paused, bracing. "We might not be alone, right?"

"Not alone?" Caleb said, puzzled.

"Not the only ones who want to take the system down," Eric said, returning briefly to his usual bluntness.

"The possibility is definitely there," Dave said, turning the thought around in his head.

"Maybe," Caleb agreed. "But how many are there? And how effective could they be?"

"That's for us to find out," Eric said, half a smile appearing on his face.

"You mean we go out there and ask wanna-be Power Engineers if they want to join us on our quest to bring down the tyrannical government that's ruling us?" Dave said, forcing himself not to laugh.

"Pretty much." Eric nodded, maintaining a straight face. "Think about it. How many of them might be as scared as we are of speaking up? If we show them they're not alone, we might gather some numbers. Not very much, but it'll be more significant than three."

"You sound like Ashe," Caleb said quietly, almost whispering.

"That sounds too logical for me to refuse, so..." Dave said, sitting up and slapping his thighs.

The three junior Power Engineers looked at each other, each switching eye contact between the other two, and as the three stared at each other, their bond together grew stronger. First, youngsters with common interests, now brothers-in-arms fighting a war behind the luxurious doors of the Engineer Training Facility.

So far, they had seen information and logs concerning too many topics for them to keep count, but they tracked the most significant ones, which included the power distribution files Dave had seen the first time.

Dave, as the only one able to communicate with the computers of the data center's database owing greatly to his Networks course, had always been the only one inside. Eric and Caleb were usually lookouts. So, since his first trip to the data center with Caleb, Dave had visited the data center whenever he could. The facility's sophisticated computers, however, were not unprotected, and surveillance cameras were installed in the special room, and that soon made a mask or any covering for his face a requirement to enter the room.

"You know what we could use, too?" Caleb said suddenly.

"What?" The other two turned to him, Eric leaving the screen and Dave leaving his notebook.

"The data center's surveillance," Caleb said with a small smile. "They are proud enough to keep guards off campus despite the fact that they're getting hacked. That's more and more disgusting."

Eric and Dave stared at him blankly for a while.

"What do you mean?" Eric said, his mind still focused on the tasks he'd looked away from.

"We've infiltrated the place quite five or six times by now," Caleb said. "Their computers record it when someone logs in to view the data, so they know someone's been looking at their database since our first visit. Dave keeps them from locating the port, but he can't stop the log being recorded since that is in the machine, right?"

"Yes," Eric followed, his focus shifting bit by bit from his tasks to Caleb.

"Now, they must secure all the places through which the database can be accessed," Caleb went on. "No one on the outside should know about the database except for the engineers dealing with it. So, their only suspects are on campus. Yet, they still haven't put guards on the room."

"I never noticed that, actually," Dave said, a smile slowly appearing on his face.

"Me neither," Eric said, then he turned to Caleb. "You're right."

"We're above guards' supervision, huh?" Dave said musingly.

"Yep," Caleb affirmed scornfully. "They can't disturb the peace and harmony of the educational campus."

"Student logs, then," Dave blurted.

"Student logs?" Caleb said.

"They have logs of our names and backgrounds recorded in the data center as well," Dave explained. "I saw them a couple of times back. They should help us narrow down who we want to talk to instead of going around and endangering ourselves by asking everyone in person."

"Background is insignificant, though," Eric stated powerfully.

The other two raised an eyebrow.

"I'm from the Enclave," Eric said matter-of-factly. "Would you expect me to be here?"

The other two looked at each other and shrugged.

"So, what now?" Caleb said, hiding his frustration.

"We can check the backgrounds anyways, just in case," Eric said, noticing Caleb's dissatisfaction. "They might give us some leads, at least."

"Guys," Dave demanded the other two's attention with his voice. "Careful. This one's a little tougher. Student logs are the second biggest part of their database. This visit's going to take a bit longer."

"Have you looked at them before?" Eric said.

"When I was passing by last time," Dave said. "I caught a glimpse, and it was pretty big."

"Let's define our objective, then," Caleb said.

"We're looking for other students who we might be able to convince to join us," Eric said. "Or maybe we can find some friends."

"Can you look at the other students' grades?" Caleb said, his eyes widening as he turned to Dave.

"Yeah, why?"

"There might be a dissatisfied student here," Caleb said, a vicious look taking over his eyes. "Or someone who's about to fail out. Too bad we can't promise them anything because we can't edit the data."

Eric and Dave looked at Caleb silently for a while as if staring into his soul.

"No," Dave declared bluntly.

"What?" Caleb was stunned by the refusal. The trio's main objective so far had been to stay out of sight and try to keep their antics under wraps so they could survive. Numbers would make that easier. When nearly everyone around them was in on the scheme, it would be easier to blend into the crowd and move more swiftly.

"We're not doing that," Dave said, confidently holding himself upright and focusing his eyes on Caleb. "That wouldn't make us any better than them, and it might count as blackmail. We're trying to gather numbers out of thin air. We need people we can trust and, like Eric said, friends. We're discussing this right now because we trust and value each other. If we gather an army of drones who just want better grades, we won't get anywhere. We might get in even more trouble. Besides, how does it make sense to strive for better grades if the whole point is to bring down the system, grades, and everything?"

Caleb stopped for a second as his words dawned on him for the first time. Caleb realized he had sunk low enough to want to manipulate students' grades as an incentive for them to join a movement against the government. A hunger for power screamed inside, leaving Caleb wondering why he had thought like that in the first place. Ashe would not have been proud. The point of defying the system was to bring forth a better world, not take down their enemies. So, as Caleb looked between his friends, he took a deep breath and reflected on his words.

"Quality over quantity, so to say," Eric said.

"Yeah," Caleb said, the room around him partially coming back into focus. "Yeah, you're right."

"Don't worry," Eric said knowingly as he leaned back on his chair, a subtle, soothing tone in his voice. "You're surrounded by hunger for money and egotistical competition. It's not completely your fault for thinking that way."

Guilt crept up on Caleb's heart, ready to tear him apart. "I didn't mean to..."

"Don't lose sight of our actual goal in the middle of all this chaos," Eric said soothingly. "You were inspired to act because of their injustice. Don't let it infect you."

Dave stood up and waved his hand in front of Caleb's face as if checking to see whether he was conscious while Caleb fell into his thoughts. Flashbacks of Ashe and their bike chases late at night ran through Caleb's head.

What would Ashe do? Caleb thought again. *Why do I always think that? I have to find him somehow.*

"Is Ashe flashing back again?" Dave teased.

Caleb poked him in the shoulder and grunted.

"You're back online." Dave, smiling, slapped him on the back.

"We're all set, then?" Eric said with the same soothing tone as he looked Caleb in the eye. As the silence hung between the two, Caleb could sense Eric's unspoken concern. In moments like these, words were unnecessary. The trio's intuitive understanding of each other's intentions was strong enough.

"Yeah," Caleb said, his voice filled with a mixture of affirmation and subtle reassurance. He nodded and shared a long look with Eric. "I'm okay."

A few seconds later, a knock on the door interrupted the friends' peaceful silence.

"Yes?" Eric said, keeping his distance from the door.

A formal, male, oddly familiar voice called from behind the door, "Mr. Eric Mitchell?"

"This is him," Eric responded coldly, staying where he was.

"May I come in?" The voice had a shrill quality about it, which annoyed the three.

Caleb and Dave both stood with furrowed eyebrows, trying to remember the voice's owner.

"Is that the guy who brought us in on...?" Dave realized out loud.

In his confusion, Dave had forgotten to lower his voice, and his question was loud enough to travel. Caleb slapped his hand down over Dave's mouth before he could keep talking.

"Calm down," Caleb commanded, his hand not moving off Dave's mouth. "Yes, that's the guy who brought us in on the first day."

Dave's eyes were still wide with the realization.

Eric watched the two with a mixed expression of entertainment and embarrassment and a barely contained laugh.

"May I?" Eric said, raising an eyebrow and letting out a small sigh as he gestured at the door.

"Yes," Caleb said as he took his hand off Dave's mouth, and the sound of gasping started again.

"What do you think he wants?" Dave turned to Eric. A warning look appeared in Dave's eyes as he gestured toward himself and Caleb.

Eric's confidence burst forward, and a cold calmness took over his face. "Let's find out."

4

AMBASSADOR

"Ashe!" Aaron's voice boomed through the building's entrance.

"What is it?" Ashe rushed in with Hunter on his tail. Ashe came upon a wall of men standing in the entrance to receive him. Aaron and Nolan stood in the middle.

"Oh, no," Ashe thought out loud. Aaron's crowded meetings usually meant bad news.

"Big news," Nolan said happily.

Ashe's eyes widened with hope. "Well, what is it?"

"Verdantia wants you," Aaron said, and silence dropped onto the scene.

"What?" Hunter's eyebrows furrowed on their own as he came closer, and his neck craned forward.

"We've caught the attention of the rulers of the Verdantia Dominion," Aaron said formally. "They're sending their president to meet us, but they want to meet with someone who represents us. A leading figure, they said."

"How did you learn about this?" Ashe asked as he stood with his arms folded, his back straight, and one hand raised to hold his chin.

"One of the guards broadcast it on the street with a loudspeaker," Aaron said.

"Streets," one of the men corrected. Ashe recognized him as the farmer who'd come to him saying he was willing to fight.

"They left after that," Aaron said abruptly.

"Who left?" Hunter's initial confusion was still unanswered. "What's going on?"

"The guards broadcast on the streets today that the ruler of Verdantia is coming to the Hollows, which is probably because of us," Aaron said. "Anyways, they want us to choose one of us to represent us in the meeting with Verdantia's ruler."

Silence prevailed, and all eyes fell on Ashe, who looked around confused, still processing what he'd heard.

"Verdantia wants you, man," Hunter said, breaking the silence. His smile was proud, but his eyes remained worried.

"I just came here a month ago," Ashe said. "How am I supposed to represent the Hollows?" Ashe's voice, for the first time, had doubt in it.

"What do you mean a month?" Nolan said after a pause filled with everyone's awkward silence. "You've been doing all of this, and now, you come and tell us you're new. Get ready, kid, you're meeting the president of Verdantia."

"Wait, wait, wait," Hunter said, putting his hands between Ashe and the wall of men standing around Aaron and Nolan. "How do we know they're serious? We're Outcasts, after all. There's no way we're significant enough in their eyes for this to happen."

"The guards left," Aaron stated coldly.

"So what if they left?" Hunter argued. "They never used to show up in the first place. This might be an empty threat. Something to make us behave for a while."

"They completely pulled out." Nolan put his hands on Hunter's shoulders, holding him in place. "Even the ones who lounged around. Those days are gone, Hunter. We're different now."

Hunter looked up at Nolan with anxious eyes, showing his friend a glimpse of his worry.

"They didn't set a time for the meeting either," one of the men said. "It might be a message telling us to get prepared."

Ashe and Hunter looked at each other with grim expressions.

What's going on? Ashe's mind screamed.

"Where is the closest place we can contact the guards?" Ashe said, taking the lead of the situation and pushing Hunter's hand away from him.

"The District Office downtown," Nolan answered. "But no one goes there."

"Why? Out of disgust?" Ashe answered his question before he could ask it.

"That's right, Mr. Walker," the two men who spoke before said in unison with a third man, all standing on Aaron's right. "Because that's how we should deal with them."

Their enthusiasm cheered Ashe up and set the room alight. However, it couldn't compete with the anxiety in the air. The government had made it personal.

"I don't think we should do anything," Ashe said, forcing his mind to take over instead of his emotions. "Right now, at least. We must be smart about this. They might be coming to inspect us and see where we stand."

"Keep us in check, you mean?" another man spoke.

"Exactly," Ashe said with a nod. "We have to be clever about this. We can't let anything slip, or else we don't know what they'll do. Let's do a status check just to make sure we're okay." Ashe looked at the men around him. Everyone automatically stood facing Ashe, and all eyes centered on him as he spoke. "Where are we, in other words?"

"We have classes for carpentry, farming, plumbing, and electricians at school," Hunter said, starting off the reports.

"I have twenty-six students," Nolan offered.

"I teach farming, sir." A man with a large beard blushed as he looked at Ashe. "But I'm sorry, I don't know how many students I have."

"It's okay," Ashe said reassuringly. "We just need to know what we have going on right now. The headcount won't matter in the long run anyways."

"I teach plumbing, Mr. Ashe," a tall, frail man said. The man's figure was so thin that his clothes looked like they hung upon his skeleton. His eyes were weathered as if exhausted by their time alive, and he had a generous head of hair and a full beard. A cool nature spread in the air around him.

Ashe nodded in response.

"We teach electric," a group of four said in unison.

The four looked oddly alike, which tickled Ashe's memory. He remembered something about four brothers who taught together at the school. Owing to the growing populace he had gotten to know, Ashe had started forgetting bit-by-bit those he didn't see frequently, and he felt ashamed for not knowing everyone by name, unlike his first few weeks when he was all active, going around and socializing with everyone he met.

"Yes, you're the Henderson brothers," Ashe said with a welcoming smile as his finger waved in their general direction. "It's a great honor to meet all of you. Your students have said the kindest things in your favor. You truly are great teachers."

"The honor is ours, sir," the four said in unison again. Their high necks and broad faces made them an imposing wall for anyone who saw them from near or far.

"I teach carpentry, in case you didn't know," Nolan said, folding his gigantic arms.

"That's staff, pretty much," Aaron stated. "HR work is done."

"Wow," Ashe whispered to himself. *Are we that short on staff? No wonder we had problems a week ago. We need to get more manpower.*

"Financials?" Hunter said.

"We're supposed to reach out to one of the head merchants who controls the city's marketplace, but that's still pending," Ashe said. "We're still short on most resources."

"The guards' arrival was actually a break from the chaos of the last week or so," Aaron said, the crowd's attention turning to him. "And we harvested some crops, so food was somewhat covered for a few days."

"That's good," Ashe said after a pause. "We're getting somewhere!" A smile slowly grew on his face as he started formulating ideas. "This might actually be the answer. We can shift our focus, all of us, to farming so we can secure the food for now. The guards didn't seem to mind it while they were here, so the president's guard might not."

"It's not subtle either, so it's a good test to see if they want to leave us alone or stir up trouble," the bearded farming teacher said, smiling as he ran his fingers through his beard.

"Great!" Ashe said, with some excitement in his voice. "We can pause the teaching at this point. We need to take stock of what we can plant right now. If we can focus on that, we can prepare for the next big move."

"Consider this carefully, though," Hunter warned. "You're talking about planting enough crops to feed the entire town."

"No, I'm talking about growing enough to feed the town and sell to the merchants," Ashe corrected, his confidence beaming from his face.

"Can we produce that much?" Aaron said, raising a corner of his mouth in doubt.

"If we all work together," Ashe said, maintaining his strong smile and trusty attitude, which always won the crowd over. "We have more than enough soil, and we all know that." Ashe looked around at the men standing around him. "For those who still haven't learned about farming, we can teach them the basics they need so they can help those who know what they're doing until they can work on their own later on."

"Yes, sir."

The man's jolly attitude infected Ashe so much that he couldn't help but smile.

Despite the tension in the air, the unity in the room made Ashe feel as powerful as ever. Influential citizens of the Hollows rallied behind Ashe in this trying time, and his opinion took precedence. The challenge of having a government representative come to the Hollows was intimidating, but Ashe felt confident going in with these people behind him. They supported him with all they could and believed in his dream.

***

"That escalated quickly," Ashe laughed as he leaned back against a wall in the school's hallway.

"You should've already known," Hunter said. "We're not just complimenting you when we say you work hard. In fact, you work too hard. You're mostly here at the school, but you have stuff going on all around the Hollows, whether you want to or not. That boy Harry and his friends are a prime example. You need to realize how much impact you have."

"I'm still not sure about that government visit thing," Ashe admitted. "We've all been working pretty hard the past month, but I didn't think it would be enough to attract this much attention. I mean, what happened? We grew some crops in our gardens that could barely last our families a week. Traffic might be the most significant change. My first week here had long walks on empty roads. Now, the streets are full of people. I know it's not like we're doing demonstrations, but we've made some changes."

"You're right," Hunter said. "We're not exactly causing major trouble. The most we're doing is crowding the streets a little, but they know better than to just ignore that.. This is how it starts. That's why they're afraid. The guards came here because of the suspicious mood of the people. Why did the Outcasts of this town specifically start just bustling around? Like I told you, we scare them because we're the most dangerous. And thankfully, they don't have that many eyes among us, so they don't have enough information about the inner workings of the Hollows."

Ashe looked mindfully at Hunter, computing his every word and filing them away. "I never thought it would go like that," Ashe said with a quiet smile as he looked in no particular direction. "It seems so funny now how much I hated them and how much I acted out. I was so foolish."

"How's the rebellion looking now?" Hunter said jokingly.

"A lot brighter, for one thing," Ashe admitted. "You guys do a lot more than you say you do. You're the ones actually holding this all together. All I do is talk."

"Stop that." Hunter slapped Ashe on the back of the head less than gently.

"Hey!"

"You came to the abandoned school, you prepared the building, you inspired the people, and you made me become a teacher," Hunter blurted. "Do I have to go on?"

"Come on," Ashe said, poking Hunter's shoulder with a hand that magically appeared there.

"Man, stop doing that!" Hunter jumped back in surprise.

5

ONCE, TWICE, AND A THOUSAND TIMES

"**H**ave you finished the other three rooms?" Thorn caught Max in the mansion's third-floor hallway.

"Yes, sir," Max said with a polite nod, which was all he could manage.

"Go on to your quarters for today, then," Thorn said with hatred in his voice, a sense of superiority emanating from him. "Duties are changing tomorrow."

"Yes, sir," Max repeated and stood still, waiting for his permission to leave.

"I don't like your hair," Thorn sneered.

"Yes, sir," Max repeated.

"And dress better," Thorn spat.

"Yes, sir."

"Now, go."

As Max walked away from the mansion, he revised what he had heard that day. Meetings upon meetings and something about vacation with Mrs. Thorn. The vacation news was mostly vague, owing to its novelty, but it was a thread Max liked to hold onto. His analytical engine had become a full-on log filled with records of the glimpses Max could see of Thorn's life. From talks and calls about his business and the guests it brought to the mansion to the routine of his daily life with his wife and children, who were oddly absent most of the time.

For the most part, things kept going as they usually did, without novelty. Cleaning the tiresome upper floors of the mansion quickly became a mind-numbing activity. The luxury of the mansion had recently started to lose its charm, and its stun factor was nulled by time, frequent visits, and the true secrets hiding behind it.

Before he knew it, Max had already memorized the layout of all the mansion's floors and the central chimney, which he and Nate shared the duty of. The chimney, the largest structure in the mansion, was a large network of pipes starting at the first floor's kitchen and splitting into two large lines that went through all the upper floors to the roof. All the fireplaces of the mansion's different rooms merged into the two major pipes that let the smoke out of the ceiling.

The first floor's only fireplace, the mansion's largest one, was in the kitchen, while the second floor had three fireplaces, one in each of the rooms. Since the second floor was for guest accommodations, the rooms with fireplaces were special, offering more luxury than the rest.

The third floor, which was the residence floor for Thorn and his family, had the three largest rooms in the mansion. The master bedroom showed Max a level of luxury he had never known existed. From the sheets to the floor tiles to the furniture and technology, everything was perfectly tailored for the comfort of society's chosen ones.

The son and daughter's rooms were exceptionally luxurious, yet they were mild compared to Thorn's bedroom. Each room had its own bathroom, the largest being in the master bedroom. The third floor's share of the chimney pipes all belonged to the single gigantic fireplace resting in Thorn's master bedroom. The pipe branching from that fireplace was almost as large as the main pipe on the first floor.

The fourth floor, Max's bane, was one large storage room for some of Thorn's old possessions and furniture he and his wife liked to keep. The fourth floor's ceiling was the highest in order to accommodate its contents, which ranged from long curtains to large sofas to wardrobes. Max's job on the fourth floor was to maintain the furniture's quality because everything the Thorn family owned always had to look new. The fourth floor's share of the chimney was only housing the two large pipes right before they went through the ceiling. Cleaning these two large pipes was also part of Nate and Max's shared duties.

***

"Duties changing, huh?" Nate said as he put his plate aside.

"He even gave me the rest of the day off," Max said between bites.

"Me too, but he didn't tell me why," Nate said, leaning back against the wall behind him and crossing his legs on the ground.

"No wonder we're here together, then," Max smiled.

Nate smiled back, showing his sincerity in his silence. "How's it going?" he said, arching both eyebrows and widening his eyes in curiosity.

"The most exciting thing is the vacation," Max said, setting aside his plate of bread with cheese and a few vegetables. "The two are going on some exotic trip, apparently. No details yet, though."

"It's about time they started preparing," Nate said wonderingly.

"Why?"

"You came here after their summer trip last year," Nate said. "That was about six and a half months ago. Their winter trip should be around this time of year, although they're a bit late if they're just starting preparations now."

"Is it an annual thing?"

"Once in the summer, once in the winter," Nate said carelessly. "They call it biannual, I think."

"How does it go?"

"They travel wherever they go, and we get a break from them for two weeks," Nate said.

"What's the catch?"

"We're not allowed out past the garden's walls, obviously," Nate said. "They get our supplies delivered. The real catch is that we're allowed out of here for half of the day, and Anna and company are allowed out the other half."

"Just how much technology is here?" Max thought out loud, channeling his inner Caleb.

"You're getting good at listening," Nate said, smiling calmly. "Good questions, too."

Max nodded with a silent smile that hid all his strife. A conversation with Nate was different from a conversation with Thorn, and Nate knew it, yet he admired Max's self-control.

"This is where all the listening pays off," Nate said suddenly, breaking the post-meal silence.

***

"Five more days, and we're done."

Anna's voice, coming from the second floor, caught Max's ears as he swept the staircase between the third and fourth floors, the unusual urgency of Anna's voice forcing him to pay attention.

"Do you have everything ready?" an older voice answered Anna. The voice was tired, exhausted even, and a sense of pain riddled it.

"Yes, the first floor's all set," Anna said, trying to hush her voice somewhat. "The second is almost there, too. Now, Hannah has to deal with the third, and we're done."

"Haven't you told Nate yet?" the older voice said scoldingly.

"No, I'm sorry." Max could hear Anna's shame as it stepped into the conversation. "I was just busy with the duty change and everything."

"You held the second floor before. There should be nothing keeping you busy," the older voice continued.

"I will tell him as soon as I can. I promise," Anna said.

"And the new boy, too," the older voice said, making Max raise an eyebrow.

"Nate might tell him anyway. We don't need to take that risk."

"No, the boy is too diligent," the older voice said worriedly. "He and Nate might not be meeting a lot these days, so we have to tell him as soon as we can."

"He *is* diligent," Max barely made out Anna's whisper.

"I'll be off now," the older voice said dismissively.

"Do you need anything?" Anna called out.

"No, thank you, dear."

***

"They talked about five days, getting things ready, and mentioned a Hannah," Max said as soon as he saw Nate in the quarters.

"You used to knock, right?" Nate said, feigning annoyance.

"Sorry," Max said scornfully, seeing through Nate.

"Hannah's the nurse, that's one," Nate started as he sat down and scratched his head as if warming his brain up for thinking. "Five days until Thorn's departure, probably, and I haven't a clue about getting things ready unless it has something to do with the winter trip."

"Anna said she prepared the first floor, the second's on the way, and the third was up to Hannah," Max continued. "I rarely see Hannah, though."

"Nurse's duties," Nate said, almost dismissively. "She stays in the quarters most of the time. Days on end, sometimes weeks."

Max's analytical engine kickstarted on its own. "How do they know she's going to get to the third floor in five days?"

"That's probably part of the preparations they're getting ready," Nate guessed.

"Oh, and they said they were going to tell us, too," Max added.

"Then, we only had to wait, and we'd have found out the rest, no?" Nate teased.

"You were the one who told me to listen," Max teased back, pointing at Nate's chest.

"I didn't mean to other Servants," Nate said with a raised eyebrow and half a smile.

Max's mind stuttered, then stopped at the word Servants.

Other Servants, Max thought, all his focus turning to the word. *We're Servants. The second lowest Stratification of society. The lowest here in the cities, at that. Society....*

"Did you see Servant kids at your Crowning?" Max said a while later as the two lay down to rest after their evening meal of pasta and some fruit, which both had found to be the most luxurious meal they'd ever had.

"Say that again. I'm still thinking about the pasta," Nate said with a warm smile.

"Did you see Servant kids at your Crowning?" Max's analytical engine couldn't lose focus.

"Not many, why?" Nate said, adjusting his pillow.

"I don't think I saw any at mine," Max said, the horrific drawing scene flashing back into his head.

"I don't know much about other Servants if that says anything," Nate said after a pause.

"You do know someone who was raised Servant, right?" Max remembered Nate's story.

"I guess," Nate said, consciousness escaping him as he spoke.

"The pasta was good, wasn't it?" Max said, happiness jumping around his stomach.

"I haven't eaten anything like that since school," Nate said.

Max stayed silent at his tongue slip, noticing Nate had noticed, and went back into his thoughts.

"Do you have any more questions?" Nate said.

I do ask too much, "No. You can go to sleep if you want to. You probably need some rest after that duty change."

"That's a joke of a duty change if you ask me," Nate spoke a little too openly for himself. "I held the entire chimney for years before you came along to share for a few months, and now I'm back where I was. All I had to do for these few months was dust some old, unused furniture. You've got to be kidding me."

"Come on, man," Max said slowly, watching Nate's head as it fell onto the pillow. "You got to take a break for a few months. I'd be thankful if I were you."

Max watched himself with amazement as he talked Nate to sleep.

"A break, huh? You should've seen what happened during Anna's initiation..." Nate laughed, a hint of consciousness still on his face.

"Really, is that another story?" Max said with the same slow tone.

Am I really doing this? Max thought, both confused and surprised.

"Yeah, maybe I'll tell you that one when..." Nate drifted off on his right side, in a perfect fetal position, hands closed on his chest.

He looks so at peace, Max thought with tears welling in his eyes. *What could he have seen so far in his life that he's that happy about a plate of food? Is killing really the wrong decision? What could Nate have gone through?*

In the heat of his own thoughts, Max drifted off himself, vowing to avenge Nate and to find Ashe. Despite Max's anger and frustration with the reality of servitude, salvation felt close. In dreams, Max's mind formed images of Ashe out of memory, hoping he wouldn't forget his first true friend.

6

ENGINEER RECRUITS

"Hello, trainee Engineers. Did you miss me?" Mr. Smith, who had led Caleb and company here on their first day, stood outside the door.

"Mr. Smith...?" Eric tried, digging through his mind to remember the stylish black suit.

"Oh, how long it's been, the pride of Greenwood," he said. The celebratory tone quickly became overbearing, and its noise was more than a nuisance.

"Greenwood?" Caleb whispered to himself, trying to recall the word.

"Greenwood Engineering Training Grounds." Dave lightly hit Caleb's arm. "We're training for Verdantia's capitol, remember?"

"Greenwood's the capitol. We're..." Signals went off in Caleb's head, and shortly, he recalled what he needed.

"Are you okay?" Dave said worriedly.

"Yeah," Caleb said dismissively.

"Where's Sophie?" Mr. Smith's intrusive voice filled the room.

The trio looked at him with raised eyebrows.

"The student you came here with on your first day."

"Oh, her." Eric tried putting on an act to humor Mr. Smith, but he was wildly unsuccessful. "We haven't seen much of her since we started training."

"Sophie..." Caleb's mind started rifling through memories again. "She said something about training underground, I think."

"That starts next year, Mr. Harrington." Smith waved enthusiastically. "Don't get too hasty now."

Does he still know my name? Caleb thought.

"To what do we owe this wonderful visit?" Eric said with a polite smile.

"Oh, how you've grown," Smith said, apparently enjoying the warmth of the situation only he felt. "Your first semester is almost over."

"Exams are three weeks away, yes." Eric nodded, then stayed silent to force any information he could out of the suit in front of him.

"I'm giving you a tour of the rest of the grounds!"

The trio looked at each other as if reading each other's minds.

Thinking about it, we've only been in three buildings so far, Caleb realized.

"Are you ready or not?" Smith said, demanding more than offering.

"We're going right now?" Eric said, acting shocked.

"Of course, I'm not interrupting you three studying, am I?" Smith said with a teasing wink, his voice catching the rest of the dorms' attention. "I heard you ranked in your classes. Good for you!"

"Thank you," the three said with the same tone and facial expressions as if mirroring each other.

"You're still as polite as ever, too," Smith congratulated.

"All right, we'll get ready and be out right away," Eric said with the warmest smile he could muster.

"I'll be waiting outside your dorms with your fellow classmen," Smith said, and he left.

"Let's go," Dave cheered quietly. Then, he turned to find a pair of dead faces staring at him. Dave didn't lose his energy. "We're going to explore the Depths!"

"The Depths?" the other two said in unison.

"The Greenwood Engineering Training Grounds A is comprised of two divisions," Dave said. "The first division, called the Surface, is where we are. It has the dorms, the data center, and the basic facilities, and it has all the classrooms for the first-year students. The second division, called the Depths, is underground. That's what Sophie was talking to you about. It's where the real work gets done. It's where most second and third-year classes are held, and it has more advanced technology. What's exciting is we're going to get a more holistic look. I don't understand a lot of what goes on there just from seeing the student logs in the data center."

"So, that's why we don't see second or third-years a lot," Eric concluded.

"Training Grounds A?" Caleb said.

"Yeah, what about that?" Eric followed.

"I didn't tell you this wasn't the only training ground in Greenwood?" Dave looked at Caleb and Eric with wide eyes. The two looked back without an answer, confirming their doubt.

"There are two others, B and C," Dave said, recalling what he had seen in the data center. "B looks the same as here, only a little bigger, and it has different programs like architecture and some of the softer stuff. Different facilities, of course. Slightly better-looking dorms. C is under wraps for now, and both are under the Verdantia Dominion."

"Training Grounds A houses the lifeline. How appropriate," Eric mocked.

"I'm surprised we didn't think about that, actually," Caleb said as his fingers rubbed his chin.

"Think about what?" Eric said.

"The fact that we haven't seen a single classroom related to architecture so far," Caleb said. "Computer engineering, either. We have Circuit Assembly, but that's general, right? The Resources classroom is also general. What else?"

"Most of our classes are general," Dave explained. "The first-year subjects over at B aren't the same, but they're similar. The Resources class is common between us. Computer engineering has Circuit Assembly and Networks, which I'm still telling you guys that you need to take."

"You don't want to go through hacking a database by yourself every time, eh?" Eric teased.

"No, it's useful knowledge, and we can use it later on," Dave said, showing genuine worry. "It's too late this semester, but you can still take it next term before you're lumped in with the others next year."

"We're going to stay here until next year?" Caleb groaned.

"We can have this conversation after we've toured, right?" Eric gestured at the door. "He's waiting outside, you know."

Dave went for the door right away. "Okay, let's go."

"Wait, we're not planning anything right now?" Caleb pulled Dave's shoulder.

"For now, it's just recon. We've technically just found out there's an underground part of this place," Eric answered.

"Exactly," Dave added. "And besides gathering information, maybe we can fish out a few... ahem... comrades."

Caleb stared at him for a little longer than expected. Then, after the long, awkward silence, he said, "What about second and third years? Can't we tell them?"

"Third-years are too risky since they're almost already fully fledged Professionals. There might be some hope in the second years, though," Eric answered again. "Let *me* do the socializing."

The same knock from before came at the door again, and Eric opened the door forcefully, defying the knocker.

"Ready?" Smith put on a friendly face, brilliantly hiding what's underneath.

"Let's go," Eric offered with an empty smile.

***

The Depths was about two times as big as the Surface with its four towers. The Depths had no dorms, an uncountable number of halls, and a large power plant that made up almost half of its space. The power plant produced electricity for the entire training grounds, above and below the earth, and served as a testing facility for the power engineers in training.

The plant was off-limits to first-year students like Caleb, Dave, and Eric, so to them, it stayed behind closed doors, while the rest of the Depths was more open to casual viewing. There were new classrooms, new classmates, new teachers, and some intriguing technology, but it was nothing too exciting. For a reason the trio couldn't make out, the air in the Depths felt more serious than on the Surface, harsher even. Perhaps it was the third-year students fighting for their lives against the grading point system that played a big part in the tension.

"What's up with them?" asked one of their first-year colleagues, pointing at a group of four students wearing Transport Engineer training shirts as they sped by. The shirts resembled the colorful Power Engineer shirts, but these had a different color pattern.

"That is a glimpse into your future, young man," Smith said to their colleague, foolishly trying to act wise.

Despite the annoyance on the boy's face, he humored Smith, asking questions and maintaining this nuisance of a conversation. "Second-years?"

Why is he doing this? Caleb thought as he exchanged looks with Eric and Dave, who watched the conversation carefully as well.

"These are third-year students," Smith explained matter-of-factly. "Transport Engineering is known for its demanding nature, and these students are just getting a taste of what a job in the real world would be like."

The boy's enthusiasm waned for a split second, which was enough for Caleb, Dave, and Eric to put the boy on their list. "What exactly is their specialty?"

"They design and manufacture what you drive every day," Smith said, mixing pride into his tone and his walk. "Or rather, what your parents drive." Smith darted his eyes from left to right as he drew a smile on his face, trying to be humorous. "Their specialization includes everything from what materials are required to designing the vehicles to letting them out on our streets."

Our streets?

"Must be an honor to serve our planet so greatly," the boy spoke again, maintaining the conversation despite the tense atmosphere around them.

"Indeed," Smith agreed, nodding vigorously. "However, you little geniuses are the lifeline of our nation."

The entire group, Caleb, Dave, and Eric with them, shifted their attention sharply to Smith as if intrigued by the words.

"You bring life to our vehicles, our homes, our roads, and pretty much everything. Be proud, youngsters. You serve our nation, the greatest of them all!"

A dead silence fell upon the tour group as the weight of Smith's words hung heavy on their shoulders. The trio carefully watched every member of the group huddled around them and began fishing out quite a few possible candidates for their list of fellow students who might join the trio on their mission to bring down the system—a goal that seemed too far away still.

As Caleb thought about the list and his plans with Eric and Dave, he looked around, taking in the scenery. Hundreds, maybe thousands, of students bustled around, each after their own ambitions and goals in a world constructed by their government. The grandiosity of the halls, with their never-ending pews and their pitch-perfect professors, pushed doubt into Caleb's heart and made his breath heavy. The very thought of defying such a system, so powerful and capable, seemed difficult when he was surrounded by its power.

What was Ashe thinking? Caleb wondered as doubt plagued his heart. *Guard fights and bike chases, that's all. Where is he now? If I could meet him for just a minute...*

In the midst of his doubt, Caleb slowly realized that Ashe wasn't with him. Ashe hadn't drawn Professional. He hadn't gone to the Greenwood Training Grounds. He hadn't studied how to be an Engineer or lied through the vicious competitions with the money-hungry monsters Caleb had for classmates. He hadn't even studied properly for school before the Crowning.

A shadow of worry fell on Caleb's thoughts as he imagined Ashe's fate. As Caleb remembered his bike rides with Ashe through the districts of Verdantia, he imagined biking through them again with him, but this time, with no guards chasing them. No black-clad ghosts followed them through the darkness of the night. Max soon came into the picture, riding on Ashe's right with Caleb on the left, like they always did.

Then, Caleb remembered Ashe's fire when talking about the system ever since the two had met outside the Suburbs near the small woods on the way to Wayward. Max had stood around, looking handsome as usual, gazing out at nothing in particular. It had all seemed easier back then.

So, Caleb vowed to carry on Ashe's will, but he would not be burdened with his memory. The rebellious Professional boy, of all people, knew he wouldn't get anywhere if he let his feelings control him, especially with the overwhelming challenges ahead. Then, he made another vow to search for both his friends with all the resources he had, even if it meant going to the ends of the earth.

"Caleb?" Eric whispered into his ear.

"Yes," Caleb replied quickly, pretending he wasn't spaced out as the group walked through one of the largest halls he had ever seen. He thought he heard Smith say it was where the Power Generation classes were taught. "What did I miss?"

"You went 'calculator' for like five minutes," Eric said, barely holding in his laugh. "You didn't miss much, luckily. Some history about this room, that's all."

"He spent five minutes talking about this room's history?" Caleb whispered a little too loudly.

"Is there something you'd like to share, Mr. Harrington?" Smith challenged from in front of the group, prying into Caleb with his dark brown eyes. The eyes matched the suit, emanating a dark energy that accompanied the annoying enthusiasm.

From time to time, Caleb wondered about the mystery surrounding the guides who came and left mysteriously and how they fit into their training.

Caleb stepped forward as three other students made way for him to move. "Yes, sir," he replied, his voice steady.

7

THE ENIGMA OF DESTINY

"You better hit the hay now," Hunter said with a warm smile.

"It was a long day, so I won't say no to that." Ashe smiled a little wider than he intended, his eyes barely open.

"You've got a lot going on. I'll give you that," Hunter said with a smile of quiet pride. "Better get some rest. You need it."

"Just make sure everyone gets home okay," Ashe said, pointing to the stairs leading down to the building's entrance.

"All right," Hunter promised, backing away from the doorway and allowing Ashe to close his door.

"And check on those three, too, please." Ashe's hand gestured weirdly on its own.

"All right," Hunter promised.

"And the marketplace. You need to—"

"Go to sleep, Ashe," Hunter demanded forcefully.

"I will. I will," Ashe said automatically, still barely awake with his eyes struggling to keep their lids open. "You just go to the..."

"Ashe," Hunter looked him in the eyes, paralyzing him, "go get some rest."

"Okay, okay." Ashe's hand gestured on its own again before he closed his door.

As Ashe went into his room, he examined the chamber, taking in the view one more time. The compact space, peeling paint, and flickering fluorescent flights started Ashe's entry on a high note, leaving no room for expectations. The pale, cold glow from the lamps spread across the cracked wooden floor and set the musty air alight. The kitchenette with its small stove, tiny oven, and worn countertop stood in the corner, lacking pride. Ashe's dish-washing bucket sat quietly under the kitchenette's humble sink while its twin, used to hand wash clothes, rested in the bathroom. The small rickety table was in the center of the room, untouched. The cramped bathroom with its cracked and discolored tiled floor completed the painting for Ashe, and he titled the artwork "Outcast."

When Ashe lay on the threadbare mattress, resting for the first time in a while, he recalled the Crowning and all that had happened since. The six weeks he'd spent as Outcast flashed by in a second, with Harry, Hunter, and Nolan shining through. His conversation with his father had a moment in the spotlight as well, allowing Ashe to reminisce a little about his somewhat stable past as a Worker child.

Workers were an overloaded stratification of society, striving for days on end to earn a fraction of what Professionals made without lifting a finger, yet the security of a month's pay meant the world to an Outcast. His father's pay had always been enough to feed the two of them, which Ashe was always thankful for. There had been food on the table every night. Ashe recalled it just as Dan described it. Yet, the way Workers were treated negligently bothered Ashe, fueling his defiance of the government even more.

Strangely enough, Ashe remembered Max and Caleb and was able to recall conversations with them word for word. For as long as he could, Ashe bathed in the memories of his friends as he, an Outcast, lay in the farthest place from them he could imagine. Then, the fear of their reaction came up again.

What would they think? Ashe couldn't help but wonder. *Would they give up on me? What would they think about what is happening here? Is Max okay? Where did he go?*

Questions kept running infinitely through his head with no possible answers at hand, leaving him to wonder about his friends' fate, even though it relieved him a little bit that he knew Caleb had drawn Professional and been chosen for power engineering. Although weak, a sense of pride grew in Ashe when he thought about Caleb becoming a Professional.

Eventually, Ashe's vocational initiative came to his mind. It had become obvious that the Hollows had valuable citizens and that those citizens appreciated him enough to represent them despite him only becoming one of them less than two months before.

The Outcasts were truly wondrous to him, showing him how they could not just accept their fate but embrace it with open hearts to live free of all the burdens of society. So, why were they looked down upon? Ashe pondered on them for the longest time, turning all his thoughts around in his head.

Why do they accept it, though?

The Outcasts' positivity, particularly Hunter's, was often too good to be true. Yet, something about kneeling down the way they did bothered Ashe. Accepting their fate was good, but why did they have to bow down to do so? Why did accepting their fate come with such living conditions? Murky water, rundown homes, inadequate buildings, and less than helpful "support."

For hours, Ashe lay on his bed thinking, unaware of the passage of time at all. Thoughts kept coming and going, not giving his train of thought a moment to stop and rest, and before he knew it, he fell asleep, his body giving in to exhaustion after all he'd done to it over the past few days. Ashe, thankfully, wasn't teaching any skills at the school, but he had to manage literally everything from beginning to end, including the speeches he often gave. Those were fun sometimes, but they were often intimidating with large crowds. Aaron, Olivia, and his fellow newcomers made it easier on him occasionally. As Ashe drifted off, a scene started forming in front of him.

***

The silhouette of a figure stood with a sword in its hand. The figure stood its ground mightily as if awaiting challengers. In front of the shadowy form, a monstrosity stood, holding up its shield and a sword ten times the size of his opponent. The world around him was a haze. Clouds blocked his vision from everything around him, and all he could see was the figure facing the creature before it.

"Kneel," the monstrosity spoke. It had no shape. It was simply a towering beast standing on two legs and holding its weaponry, ready to prey on the puny human it faced.

"*No,*" the small figure refused, raising his sword in defense. The small warrior's voice was oddly familiar, as though Ashe heard it every day.

"Kneel," the monster repeated, its voice shaking the world around it.

"*No!*" the human warrior's voice exploded, shaking the giant himself.

Then, the world stopped again. The warrior, sword tight in his hand, stared at the giant, and the giant stared back, holding its weapon at bay. The giant looked down at its foe as if looking down at an insect, and it raised its foot. The warrior brought down his sword and looked straight up at the oncoming foot. Then, the foot hurtled to the ground, stopping exactly on the warrior's head. Under the weight and force of the foot, the small figure stood with legs wide and hands up, fighting back.

The giant pushed down, yet it was in vain. Its foot couldn't go farther down.

"*Kneel!*" the giant commanded, shaking the world with its voice again.

"*No!*" a fiercer voice answered.

"*Kneel!*"

"*Never!*" The sword dropped from the man's hand, and he resisted with all his might.

"*Kneel!*"

*****

"Get away from who?" Hunter said, his hand magically appearing on Ashe's shoulder.

"Wha... huh...?" Ashe had barely opened his eyes before he found Hunter's face staring at him. Then, he sensed the hand on his shoulder. "Get out of here." He jerked away.

"What's wrong, man?" Hunter said, laughing.

"What *is* wrong?" Ashe asked back.

"Who were you telling to get away from who?" Hunter said, taking a few steps away from Ashe's bed.

Ashe furrowed his eyebrows and craned his neck forward.

"Might've been a dream," Hunter said casually, though his sharp eyes remained on Ashe. "I've never seen anyone dream that intensely before, though."

"What dream?" Ashe said, shaking his head. Then, he realized. "That was a dream?"

Hunter smiled cheekily. "Now you're there,"

"I..." Ashe said. He paused for a minute, letting his mind piece everything together. "There was a guy... a giant... a sword..."

Hunter silently raised an eyebrow.

"There was a guy with a sword in his hand," Ashe said decisively as if finally ordering his thoughts. "There was a giant. He had a shield."

"Okay, I'm following." Hunter nodded, starting to draw it in his mind.

"Everything was hazy," Ashe said, struggling to recall. "Like I was inside the clouds."

"And?" Hunter said, urging him to speak quicker.

"The giant asked him to kneel, and he didn't. He asked him again, and he didn't. Then, he stepped on him."

"And he was squashed?" Hunter tried, half-smiling.

"No." Ashe shook his head as he raised his gaze to meet Hunter's. "He held it."

"Held what?"

"The giant's foot and he refused to kneel again."

Hunter stared at Ashe. The two exchanged looks as Hunter started processing what he'd heard. Hunter's face changed a few times, and then he looked back at Ashe, who had been looking at him, waiting for help.

"Are you worried?" Hunter realized.

"I'm... shaken," Ashe admitted.

"You don't normally dream, huh?" Hunter said casually, trying to ease away Ashe's anxiety.

"Not at all usually," Ashe said, scratching the back of his head. "Maybe once or twice when I was kid, but not stuff like this."

"Where were you in all of that?" Hunter said.

Upon hearing the question, Ashe winced.

"At first, it was like I was watching them from a fair distance away, but when the giant raised his foot, I was sucked in. I felt like I was him. I was the guy with the sword." Ashe's voice was hollow, with a little bit of fear mixed in.

Hunter stopped, carefully considering what he wanted to say. Hunter thought, his thumb and index holding his chin.

"Were you scared?" Hunter asked finally, eyebrows raised and eyes wide.

"A little," Ashe said as if realizing it for the first time.

"Maybe it was just a bad dream," Hunter tried, using the fear as an excuse to dismiss the thought.

"What brought this on, though?" Ashe found himself shaking his head.

"Do you think it matters?" Hunter said.

"I'm not sure." Ashe struggled to form a single thought. His opinions got mixed together, and everything was hazy.

Hunter fell silent, allowing him to think.

"How's everything going?" Ashe said.

"Everything is going smoothly, just like you left it," Hunter said confidently, a smile forming on his face. "You sleep for a few hours, and you're worried about the Hollows. How cute."

Ashe pushed Hunter's shoulder.

"We do need you right now, though," Hunter said. "That's why I came for you. We need to discuss the ambassador thing and how we're going to meet them."

"Haven't they set a date or anything?"

"Still no."

"I think we need to meet with those three first," Ashe said. "They might help."

"The hostages?" Hunter said sarcastically.

"They told us all about their training, didn't they?" Ashe argued.

"That might've been... I don't know."

"We need to ask them about the higher-ups this time. Those three are young, but they must know something, especially that blond guy."

"Why him?"

"He told us the most about their training," Ashe said as if it was obvious. "Besides, he looked like he was the one who enjoyed it the most."

"That's how we know they're not lying," Hunter whispered to himself.

"Anyway, I'll get ready in a few and meet you on the way there."

"I'll let Aaron know—"

A knock on the door interrupted Hunter.

"Come in," Ashe called.

Immediately, Nolan busted the door open, panting.

"The guards are here."

8

The Shackles Shatter

The day after Max and Nate's luxurious dinner, they resumed work normally with no sign of any other special perks coming again. As the two were busy with their tasks, Anna stayed out of their sights for most of the day, and so did the older woman. The nurse, as usual, was nowhere to be seen.

Max created a counter in his head for days and set it to four. As he cleaned out the rooms, he wondered what Anna was planning. Then, his mind wandered to the older woman, who had been the keeper of the upper floors before Anna and was the most experienced of the female Servants. Max concluded she was the one who had been raised Servant and stolen the light in Nate's stories.

"What do you think you're doing?" the same old, angry voice boomed up the staircase into the room Max was cleaning.

He's here now? Max raised an eyebrow and dropped what he was doing to listen in.

"You failure of a woman!"

Thorn seemed extra angry this time. Max was too far away to hear the response.

"To your quarters right now!"

Then, hurried footsteps left the mansion.

"Shouting again," Max said when he went up to the fourth floor.

"What's new?" Nate raised an eyebrow. "What brings you here?"

"He was too loud," Max said.

Nate scanned Max from head to toe. "Are you serious?" he said, almost angrily.

"Something's wrong," Max said gravely.

"What do you want then?" Nate offered, pulling back his anger a bit and giving Max a chance.

"We need to talk to them, to the women," Max said. "It's four days away now, and they haven't told us. We have to do something before it's too late."

Nate leaned back a little, looking Max in the eye with a subtle smile. "What are they preparing for?" Nate challenged, putting his hands together in front of his waist.

"I don't know," Max admitted.

"What do you think they're preparing for?" Nate said.

"Maybe..." Max started, then stopped when he realized he knew nothing.

"Let me rephrase. What do you *want* them to be preparing for?" Nate pushed further.

Max fell silent and considered his answer.

Have I gotten too hopeful? Am I just seeing what I want to see? Max thought. *They might be talking about just another duty. What could they be really planning?* Max started formulating, and his mind went into focus mode.

"Wake up." Nate shook Max's shoulders. "You shouldn't be here in the first place. Get out of here before he comes calling for you."

"No, I was supposed to get something from here, actually. I took the opportunity since you were here," Max explained.

"Opportunity?" Nate laughed. "We live together, kid."

"I'll meet you at home, then," Max joked.

"Don't get too caught up in your dreams," Nate said as Max turned to leave. "It might just be a false hope."

"It might not," Max offered with a smile.

***

"Max!" Anna called.

"Anna?" Max turned before going into their quarters.

"Hi, Max," Anna said kindly, the humility in her voice setting his nerves at ease.

"Hi," Max said politely, keeping his worries away from his face and showing her the most relaxed expression he could.

"I needed to tell you something," Anna said hesitantly as if asking permission.

"I'm all ears." Max returned her politeness, something he always admired. Anna was the kindest person he had ever met and the humblest.

"Hannah, Victoria, and I have been discussing some things, and we wanted to let you know since Mr. Thorn is leaving in only four days," Anna said.

"Yes." Max nodded. "Nate's told me about the winter trip."

"Victoria and I have..." Anna's voice shook.

Max stayed silent, looking away to allow her to gather herself without being watched.

"Victoria and I have been discussing a plan for the past few weeks,"

Max's memories of their whispers came to mind.

"We want to escape."

Max showed no surprise, which made Anna stutter. "Did you know?"

"I'm sorry." Anna's kindness made Max's guilt worse. "I overheard you and Victoria talking yesterday about preparations, five days, and Hannah. I'm sorry I listened in without telling you. I was cleaning the stairs then."

"Oh," Anna said, trying to figure out how to react. "Um... it's okay. Don't worry about it. You actually made it easier for me. We want to get out of here right after they leave for their winter trip."

"What does Hannah have to do with it?" Max asked, suspicions running through his mind. *If they're leaving after he leaves, why would they need Hannah to do anything?* Max's analytical engine, for the first time, impressed him.

"I'll come to that," Anna said. "We want him to suspect nothing at all. We're trying to make everything look more than perfect so he isn't tipped off. The children are away, so they won't matter, and the wife goes with him."

"Was all that shouting earlier today a part of it?" Max asked carefully.

Anna blushed and said shamefully, "I was too distracted, and I dropped something in the kitchen. Victoria told me she'd do her best to handle it since she's dear to him."

"She came here about a year or so after Nate, he tells me," Max explained.

"Nate's been here for that long?" Anna said, shocked.

Max nodded.

"Anyways, before I tell you anything more, I need to know. Do you agree to help?" Anna said.

Max stopped, realizing he wasn't just listening to Nate tell him a story. Anna and Victoria needed to get out, and he especially understood why they'd want to escape. Yet, he never seriously thought of running away. It was always just a dream or a fantasy that hung around, giving them false hope. Now, things were starting to move. Could two Servants really escape their Elite masters?

"I... uh..." Max struggled to form words, overwhelmed by the stream of thoughts he had just experienced.

"I'm sorry to tell you this all so suddenly," Anna said, "but this is the earliest I could tell you."

"But why do you want to leave now after all this time?" Max asked, his curiosity piqued.

"It's become too much," Anna said after a pause, her voice filled with pain. "We can't handle this anymore. There are things that I can't tell you about."

"We're still Servants," Max said tentatively. "Where can we go?"

"Anywhere but here," Anna said confidently. "Wherever it is, it'll be better than this."

"I'm just a little confused," Max admitted, forcing himself to calm down. "When I overheard you, I thought of it as a fantasy or a dream, but I didn't think about really doing it." Then, Max asked the obvious questions, "How are you going to do it with the gates closed? How do you plan on escaping here in the first place?"

"Hannah is going to handle the gates," Anna explained. "Victoria and I are trying to make him lean on her more so she can be around him enough to eventually get his phone, which has control over the mansion's security."

Max raised an eyebrow as he rubbed his chin. He was about to ask a follow-up when she continued.

"Yes, it controls the gates, our quarters, and everything else on the property."

"That's how he removes the doorknob from the men's quarters at night?" Max said.

"And ours," Anna confirmed. "We're not allowed out when we're not needed either."

"So, it's all in the phone?" Max said, hope illuminating his eyes.

"Yes," Anna said. Then, she paused, allowing him more time to process before going on. "What we need is on the phone."

"Who was responsible for the pasta?" Max said suddenly.

"That was Victoria's idea," Anna smiled. "She wanted you to be in a good mood so you'd take in the news well."

"Thank you, and please thank Victoria," Max said, bowing his head. "I can't tell you how happy it made Nate. I couldn't imagine him being that content. I can't thank you enough."

"No need at all." Anna blushed and nodded affirmatively.

"So, what do you need from me?" Max said, his face brightening.

"We need you to behave normally as much as you can," Anna said. "And come with us. We don't want to leave you here. Nate, either."

"What happens when they come back from their trip?" Max challenged.

"They'll have lost five of their five Servants. They have to either look for new ones, which forces them to wait for weeks without anyone serving them, or they can ask the guards to look for us, which forces them to pay," Anna said.

"That still leaves us with nowhere to go."

"I've heard there are some things going on in an Outcast sector nearby. Maybe we can hide there for a while."

"Outcast?" Even the word sounded foul to Max. The absolute lowest of lows. Servant was the lowest Stratification he had seen, and it was already bad enough. No one even knew how the Outcasts lived. What would the actual worst be like when they were almost completely ignored by the government? At least the Servants got to live amongst the Elite.

"You look smart, Max," Anna said wisely, contrasting her young age. She seemed to be close to Max's age. "These Stratifications are insignificant labels they put on us to control us. You must know this by now. You can't let them get to you."

Max's mind went into overdrive as he started hearing Ashe's voice in his head. He felt like he had just heard Ashe's words coming from Anna's mouth. They shared their fierce defiance and refusal to accept the system's twisted divisions of society. The certainty in Anna's words, like Ashe, pulled Max in.

"What?" Anna said after a long, awkward pause.

"I'll help you in any way I can," Max said immediately.

"Are you sure?" Anna tested him with a raised eyebrow, listening carefully for the answer.

"Of course," Max affirmed, Ashe's spirit awakening bit by bit within him.

Confusion took over Anna's face.

"What's wrong?" Max said.

"It's nothing," Anna said, regaining focus. "I just thought I'd have to convince you more at first."

"I'm not like that," Max said, thankful for what Ashe's friendship had instilled in him. "My friends and I didn't like the system that much either before I came here."

"I'm sorry," Anna said after a pause. "I don't want to waste your time since you probably need your rest. Please tell Nate, and I'll tell you what we'll do next. You overheard us, so you know Hannah's supposed to come out in two days."

"I've actually been listening in on Thorn for a while," Max said. "I can probably help with the timing if you need that."

"Listening?" Anna raised an eyebrow.

"Spying on him," Max said bluntly, surprising Anna.

"Wow, you and your friends must have really hated the system," Anna whispered, mostly to herself.

Max pretended he didn't hear.

"We need to identify Thorn's schedule because he moves around too much," Anna said. "If you can help us with that, we'll always know where he's going."

"I can do that," Max said.

***

"They're escaping," Max said quietly as he and Nate had their dinner.

"Sounds about right," Nate joked, not taking his eyes off his food.

"Anna told me that she and Victoria have been preparing for this for a while," Max said. "They're going to get Hannah out so she can get to his phone and allow us out of the mansion when Thorn and his wife are away."

"How do they plan on getting Hannah out?" Nate said, holding back his sarcasm to listen.

"It probably has something to do with the food they prepare," Max said. "Oh, and the pasta was Victoria's idea, in case you wanted to know."

"Now, I have to thank her," Nate said to himself.

"It doesn't look like anything big, but..." Max said, then stopped to choose his words.

"There is hope." Nate smiled reassuringly. "This might be your big break, kid. You never know."

"They also said there's some stuff going on in an Outcast sector nearby," Max said. "They said we can hide there for a while until we figure out what we're going to do."

"Outcast?" Nate raised an eyebrow, caught off guard by the word.

"Yeah," Max said, looking up from his food. "I was as surprised as you are."

"You never know."

9

A NETWORK

"Why are we doing this?" Caleb asked bluntly, looking Smith in the eyes.

"To learn how you are going to serve our planet," Smith said confidently.

The touring group turned into an audience standing around Smith and Caleb, who had a safe distance between them.

"Who does 'our' refer to exactly?" Caleb said, unapologetically showing his annoyance.

Smith looked at him silently for a few seconds, measuring his response. "The nation," Smith said, hiding behind his response's vagueness.

Caleb's only response was a mocking look, which triggered some laughter in the audience.

"You are the lifeline of the nation, young man. Be proud of who you get to serve," Smith said, returning to what he intended to be a glorious speech.

"Why do we have to do this much?" Caleb said, gathering all his might and confidence where he stood. "We compete with each other over grades and numbers. Is this to decide who serves the planet best? If you want to talk about the planet, tell me how much damage we cause to mine our resources and how we're killing the environment and hurting animals. All we want is money."

Smith looked on, now without the slightest hint of amusement. His eyes were flat and devoid of any emotion.

"What do you want to say, Mr. Harrington?" Smith challenged.

"I want to say what we're all doing here is useless," Caleb announced. "We have more than enough studying to be Professionals for this to be fair. Why can't it be simpler than this?"

"Sounds to me like you're too lazy and can't catch up with your fellow students who want to serve their planet from the bottom of their hearts," Smith said with a sickly grin.

"Who here agrees with me that our studies are too hard for a regular student to follow and that we should slow down a little?" Caleb spontaneously called out to the audience, helped by the nature of the Power Generation hall they stood in. At that moment, Caleb discovered in himself confidence he never knew existed.

"I do." Eric and Dave joined right away, standing behind their friend.

Then, the crowd shifted, and the sound of whispers spread around. All the Professionals were secretly intimidated by the system despite not wanting to show it. They liked others to believe that they were an intrinsic part of the system, and although they were, they chose to go about it the wrong way, demonstrating false power and feigning influence.

"I do." The boy who was asking questions earlier stepped behind Caleb, standing side by side with Eric and Dave.

"Me too." A few more boys joined, forming a bubble behind Caleb.

"What is this all supposed to mean?" Smith said with disgust, crossing his arms and tilting his chest away.

Caleb stared at him for a while, intentionally intimidating him.

"We're starting a student activity," Caleb announced proudly, and immediately, the crowd went silent as they all exchanged looks with their friends.

Caleb knew that neither Smith nor anyone below Elite status could touch a Professional. Smith didn't look like anything short of Professional, maybe even an Enclave Professional, but he wasn't Elite. An Elite wouldn't waste time guiding Professional students around.

All Smith could do was show his annoyance and maybe go to the Training Grounds' management and ask them to keep an eye on some students. Guards were still not allowed on the grounds, which gave Caleb another advantage.

58

Student activities weren't a new concept to the Training Grounds, and they were usually considered silly, except by the ones who ran them. This would provide an excellent cover for Caleb.

"And what exactly will you be doing in this extracurricular?" Smith said, his annoyance and alertness still at their sharpest. He saw through the obvious cover of the student activity. He knew they were up to something.

"We're going to find ways to make studying less stressful for the engineering students," Caleb said confidently, seizing the moment. "We don't want to be jumping between classes, exhausted and struggling to manage one subject after the other. We're also going to help other students, whoever wants it, with their studying."

"I'm in," another few students said immediately, joining the crowd.

"We want to serve our nation. We don't want to kill ourselves for money," Caleb said, mockingly enough to be annoying but not enough to be out of the bounds of his Professional status.

"Yeah," a few more cheers came from the crowd, who started gathering behind Caleb, leaving Smith almost alone on his side, with only a few students standing around the general area he stood in.

"Then, I wish you the best of luck in your academic endeavors." Smith smiled ceremoniously.

***

"Nice work!" Dave hit Caleb's back a little too hard.

"Where did you get that..." Eric looked Caleb in the eye. "flow?"

"I don't know." Caleb shook his head as he straightened himself up, careful to be facing Dave.

"So, what do we do now?" Dave said excitedly.

"We just deal with the collateral damage, I guess," Caleb answered gravely as he sat down at his desk.

"What do you mean?" Dave's expression changed, worry replacing enthusiasm.

"I might have done too much," Caleb said. "We could've just gone around and asked them in secret instead of going out on a limb to do that."

"You did the right thing," Eric said, breaking the silence that ensued. "Talking to a few people and fishing out the right ones would've taken too much time, especially considering we have to stay afloat in our studies. We can't just be going around talking to people and ignoring our work. We wouldn't be taken seriously in the first place."

"The tutoring plan was a good point," Dave admitted, pointing at Eric.

"You attracted attention the right way," Eric said as he stepped closer to Caleb. "The student activity cover needs the right management, and you and I can do that. The few who joined should also be glad to help, especially the first ones who spoke up since they seemed to see through Smith's words more than the rest."

"That first guy was impressive, questions and all," Caleb said.

"And we can get more like him to join us this way," Eric said. "We're pretending to be a student activity when we're actually planning a rebellion. Right? That's what I understood from you."

"Yes," Caleb affirmed. "But I didn't think too much about the consequences. We're now going to have an extra hard job, studying, running this activity, and talking to people."

"Like we just said, you and Eric can do the management stuff since I'm already busy studying extra subjects and such," Dave said, joining Eric in comforting Caleb. "Besides, I don't think it's gonna be long before we're out of here."

"Out of here?" Caleb raised an eyebrow as he sat up.

"You weren't planning on staying to finish your studies before the rebellion, were you?" Dave said jokingly.

"What do you mean?" Caleb was still confused.

"It looks like things have started moving. There's apparently some action going on in an Outcast sector in Verdantia," Dave explained.

"You heard about that, too?" Eric turned to Dave.

"Yeah, my parents told me," Dave said.

"Mine too," Eric added.

"Why am I always the last to find out between the three of us?" Caleb said annoyedly.

"Better than not knowing at all, no?" Dave tried, a smile on his face.

"Your parents should call you later this week. They might tell you themselves," Eric said, not realizing Caleb was still stuck on one word.

"Outcast?" Caleb said, his eyebrows furrowed. "Since when do we ever hear about them? I don't think I saw any Outcast children at our Crowning either."

"They're calling it suspicious activity," Eric said. "Like you said, we don't hear about them often, which makes it interesting."

"What? You think there's rebellious activity going on there?" Dave said bluntly.

"Why go that far?" Caleb questioned the idea right away.

"The lowest Stratification doesn't usually call for much attention," Dave explained. "My dad tells me security is moving around there pretty heavily."

"What do you suggest we do then?" Caleb said, the thought of Outcasts still fogging his mind. He had always known them as the lowest Stratification of humanity, not even worth being integrated into society, thus left out of everyone else's matters and left to live in exile on their own outside the main cities.

Despite his hatred of the system and his general acceptance of Stratifications as oppressive labels created by the system, Outcasts still felt distant, his Professional upbringing playing a big part in his feelings.

"We call out as loud as we can, and we gather as many people as possible," Eric decided.

"And do what?" Caleb said, raising both eyebrows.

Eric stayed silent, trying to think of an answer.

"Demonstrations?" Dave suggested, dragging the other two's attention to him.

"No," Caleb and Eric said in one voice. "Not in a million years."

"Why not, though?" Dave said, shaking his head. "We can pressure them to do what we want since we're Professionals and all."

"Remind me. What is it that we want to accomplish?" Eric said scornfully.

"A just world that doesn't discriminate by Stratification." Dave counted with his fingers. "Better living conditions for everyone."

Eric laughed out loud, interrupting Dave's list. "Who are you kidding?"

"We need a new system," Caleb said, sympathizing with Dave after hearing Eric's harsh laugh. "They'll just bribe us with more money or better jobs since we're Professionals. That won't work. We need something effective. We need to communicate with the world. We need to get out of the Training Grounds."

"You can't get off the Training Grounds before exams. That's point number one," Eric said. "Two, how loyal do you expect the people we gather to be?"

"We have to make it clear how serious we are from the get-go, then," Dave said. "We're trying to bring the government down and all."

"That's it!" Caleb jumped onto his feet. "We need to communicate with the world." The two looked at him with wide smiles, waiting to listen to the rest. "We need to get to the other Stratifications."

"You're going to go around in a Jeep calling for rebels?" Eric said scornfully.

"Not at first, no," Caleb said, hope lighting his eyes and excitement appearing in his movement. "We have to start acting as soon as we can get out of here, and once we do, we can't come back."

"It's risky."

"So, what?" Caleb's spirit went to a high. "If we're trying to bring an end to this, a shortage of Professional students might just be the start." Then, Caleb looked at Eric and Dave. "But we have to leave a mark. We can't just sit on the sidelines after finding out what we have."

"Sounds great," Eric said, speaking seriously for the first time in what felt like a while. "But how are you going to do that? You are completely surrounded. You have nothing to do in life but the role assigned to you. You are a Power Engineer whose job is to help the nation prosper. You do not care about any Stratifications other than Elite because the rest are below you, and you are better than them. So, how do you speak on behalf of others?"

Faced with the real caliber of the challenges, Caleb fell into thought, trying to formulate a plan or to think of anything that could help their situation. He also kept in mind that what Eric had stated wasn't the only challenge they faced. The harder challenge would be the guards.

The government's brutal armed forces took out anyone who dared defy the system and made them an example. The government's guards were the only ones allowed to bear arms under any circumstances, making them the only defenders of the nation and its citizens and simultaneously their prison wardens.

Caleb's mind went back to Ashe again. What would he do? Ashe knew how brutal the guards were, and he had experienced it firsthand, yet he'd never given up. Where was he?

"How about we take a risk?" Dave said, breaking the grim silence that fell for a few very long minutes.

The two looked at him, hope shining in their eyes.

"How about we go to the Outcasts?" Dave said quickly. Then, he paused to give them a moment to process his idea.

"I know," he interrupted before they could speak. "It sounds dangerous and weird, and we're all afraid of the unknown, but think about it. Why are the Outcasts always brushed away and left alone and outside of society? Why are they always exiled far away from everyone else, especially the government? We know it's not because they're outlaws because people have to draw Outcast. You don't become an Outcast because of a crime you've committed."

When Dave saw Eric and Caleb listening intently, he continued, "There must be something about them that makes them too dangerous to keep around regular people."

"Dangerous," Eric and Caleb echoed.

"The 'suspicious activity' Dad's been telling me about might be something exciting, don't you think?" Dave's face shone the brightest it ever had. Then, after a pause, he said, "So, what do you think?"

"We're going to meet some Outcasts."

10
WHISPERS

T hree months had passed since it was announced that the Verdantian president would be visiting. For the first few weeks, they spread the farming trades among the Hollows' citizens as quickly as possible, as covertly as possible. Slowly, the entire town turned into farmers, struggling to maintain their illusion.

Bit by bit, Ashe sunk into the role of ambassador as he met with the citizens of the Hollows even more than before, whose belief in him had only grown. The guards stayed completely out of sight the entire time, leaving everyone on high alert at every second, wondering why they weren't there. Yet, the Outcasts of the Hollows were smart enough to know that their absence was calculated, and it didn't mean they weren't being watched.

Hunter, Aaron, and Olivia finally got a break when classes at the school slowly died out and spread throughout the city instead.

"Thanks, Ashe," the bearded farming teacher said as he left.

"See you tomorrow, kid," Nolan said as he closed the door behind him.

Ashe sighed in relief right after the door closed. "That was something."

"You should expect nothing less," Hunter said, his eyes scanning what used to be the principal's room. "We told you how to speak. You added what you're going to say. Now, all we need to do is prepare as best we can."

"Too bad we can't prepare any other way," Ashe said with a dull voice as he leaned back in his chair, tapping the ravaged wooden desk with his fingers.

"More than a few talked to me about that, actually," Hunter said, turning to Ashe. Hunter's arms were folded over his chest, and one hand was rubbing his beard. "Getting ready to fight and all."

"It shows great spirit," Ashe said wisely, "but they're not reading the situation correctly."

"As in?" Hunter said.

"They've seen what they think is their savior, and they're blinded by that image," Ashe said, worry creeping into his voice. "They don't see we're more in need than they are."

"That's an interesting way to put it," Hunter said wonderingly. "They do like you, and they are willing to help you with all they can. Where do you think they're going?"

"Somewhere good, I'm hoping," Ashe said, crossing his arms over his chest and fixing himself in his leaned position to stare at the ceiling. "It's been a little monotonous lately."

"Don't let your guard down," Hunter warned right away. "Ever."

"I'm not. I just want something exciting to happen," Ashe said, feeling somewhat guilty for thinking it. "I mean, the only thing that can pass as exciting right now is the talks we have with Peter, Finn, and Mike."

"They're a special case, they are," Hunter reminisced happily. "You think we should go again this week? It looks like they're on the edge, and we just need to push 'em."

"Playing it slow seems to be working for now. Let's stick with that," Ashe said confidently, showing patience Hunter hadn't seen in him before.

"*He* could come anytime, you know," Hunter said, the usual worry taking over his face again.

"We already know they're watching us," Ashe said. "We can't let them know we're ready until we are. I've been practicing a lot with everyone, but I don't think we're anywhere near where we need to be."

"To fight, you mean?" Then, Hunter raised a teasing eyebrow. "Are you intimidated?"

"A bit," Ashe admitted, ignoring the mockery. "It's easy to talk big, but once you're really there, the world seems a lot different. I'm still eighteen, you know. Freshly Crowned."

"Freshly? The world seems different?" Hunter said, standing incredibly still as he stared at Ashe with his eyebrows twitching as he tried to keep a straight face. "Who are you, and where's Ashe Walker?"

"Seriously?" Ashe said, still leaning back and looking at the ceiling.

"What do you mean the world seems different?" Hunter said forcefully as if trying to beat it into Ashe. "We're both here. Everyone's still around. Everything is mostly the same way. What revelations have you had that changed everything?"

"Maybe sitting with you guys all this time," Ashe said half-jokingly.

"Those farmer guys are pretty wise, yeah," Hunter said weakly.

"Nolan's a big part of it if I'm being honest," Ashe said quietly. "You too, man."

Hunter stopped, setting the compliment aside for the moment. "So, what changed?"

"I had another dream."

***

"Start at the beginning," Hunter said.

"Obviously," Ashe said, raising a scornful eyebrow.

Hunter shot him a look. "Just go on," he said kindly, showing Ashe the warm support he needed.

He knew firsthand how stressed Ashe was and how he felt burdened by the people's expectations. Ashe's sleep pattern was a nightmare, even to Hunter, who had grown up Servant and lived in the Hollows for longer than he could remember. He often thought Ashe worried too much or worked too much, and he voiced his thoughts sometimes, but Ashe rarely listened. The last time Hunter remembered Ashe sleeping properly was two months ago, before Ashe told him about the dream with the giant.

So, he looked at Ashe, waiting for his thoughts to spill out and illustrate his dream, but Ashe struggled to speak. He seemed to be at a loss for words.

"Take it easy," Hunter said soothingly. "Draw the picture first. Where were you? When was it?"

"Same as last time," Ashe said eventually. "A hazy place among the clouds. Hazier than last time, though. Darker. More ominous."

"Time?" Hunter stressed to remind Ashe.

"I don't really know. Maybe it was nighttime since it was so dark." Ashe stared at the ground. "The clouds were thicker, too. Everything was wrapped in their gray fluff as if the whole world was soft."

Grey fluff? Hunter thought as he scratched his head.

"They moved slowly, forming the void we were in," Ashe said after a pause. "We floated more than stood on their surface and glided more than walked."

We? Hunter thought as he furrowed his brows.

"Who else was there?" Hunter said, speaking mostly to let Ashe know he was there to help. "Was it the giant and the little guy again?"

"That's just relative," Ashe said. "The smaller one was like my size."

"So, little," Hunter said, barely holding his laugh.

Ashe silently smacked Hunter's shoulder with zero hesitation.

"Hey!" Hunter said, although not as loudly as Ashe expected.

"The man held his sword like last time, and he stood his ground," Ashe said. "And the other monster, the giant, was also there. This time, he only had his shield. The two squared off like last time. Giant asked Man to kneel a few times, Man refused, and he stepped on him again."

"And?" Hunter said, knowing there was more and hating Ashe for stopping where he did. "What made this time different?"

"For starters, it was tighter. I couldn't breathe that well," Ashe said.

"And it was darker," Hunter added, receiving a nod from Ashe. "But you didn't mention anything about breath last time."

"I didn't have to think about it last time," Ashe said gravely, his eyes widening with fear. "This time, he looked at me."

"Which one?" Hunter said, annoyed by the vagueness but sympathizing with Ashe's shaken state.

"Giant," Ashe barely mouthed it. His face contorted subtly, betraying his raw fear. His irises dilated as if trying to take in every detail of what he saw. Sweat glistened on his forehead, reflecting the trepidation within. His eyebrows arched upwards, deeply furrowing his forehead, while his lips, barely noticeable, quivered, and his jaw tightened, adding to his tension.

"What did he look like?" Hunter thought of the simplest question he could.

"Horrible," Ashe blurted, fear still in his voice and on his face. "He had a helmet on with horns shooting out and up, each horn about as big as me. The helmet's metal was pitch-black, absorbing every trace of light around it. A slit ran down the center of the helmet, and it showed nothing on the inside. Just emptiness. And his eyes..."

Hunter wrapped his arms around Ashe's shoulder and hugged him tight. Ashe had been shaking more violently than he thought, and fear had consumed him. Hunter's warmth comforted Ashe a bit, easing some words out of him.

"His eyes?" Hunter said, urging Ashe to finish his story, to let it all out.

"After he asked Man to kneel, and he stepped on him again, Man held the foot like last time. The sword dropped again, but Man didn't. As Giant tried to push him down, he stopped and turned to me, his foot still on Man. Then, he opened his eyes."

Ashe quivered. "They gleamed with an intensity I've never seen, like molten gold. The irises burned with an overwhelming radiance as if they could peer into my soul. The pupils, were mere pinpricks of darkness. Right then, I shivered. The predatory glimmer... it was evil."

Hunter silently wrapped his other arm around Ashe, getting him in a full hug to calm his shaking.

"So, they didn't look at you last time?" Hunter said after a long pause, knowing that he had to ask the logical questions sooner or later and that sooner was better since Ashe seemed to remember it well.

"It was like I was watching from a screen the first time," Ashe explained as he slowly broke free of Hunter's tight hug. "This time, I was with them. I could almost swear Man saw me at first, but I couldn't really tell. He didn't talk. He didn't even move his lips, but it felt like he asked for help."

"That sounds vivid," Hunter noted. "This time more than the last, obviously."

"Vivid doesn't begin to describe it," Ashe said. "I felt like I was Man. I felt the foot's weight on my shoulders. I felt everything, the wide legs, the muscles contracting, and I tried to push the foot up. Something told me I had to, like a whisper."

"Did you switch between Man and yourself?"

"Sort of." Ashe scratched his head, not really knowing himself. "One moment I was here, one moment I was there, and back again. But I couldn't control it. It just happened."

Hunter stared at Ashe, deep in thought.

"What?" Ashe said, quickly worried by the look.

"We've got to ask someone about this."

11

MASTER AND SERVANT

"Two days away!" Max celebrated as he danced into the quarters.

"Get off your high horse already," Nate said. "Anna already told you two days ago."

"Don't tell me you're not as excited," Max said, staring at Nate.

Kid's acting weird, Nate sang in his head, considering Max's unusual demeanor. Max was usually the quiet type. He was the quietest of the quiet type, yet his enthusiasm had gone through the roof since Anna told him about the plan. A rebellious fire burned bright inside Max, and he liked it so much that all he could think about was what he was going to say to Ashe and Caleb when he met them outside. Occasionally, his analytical engine questioned his logic, considering said logic involved going into a Professional sector unasked for, as a Servant, nonetheless.

"Sorry, I got a little carried away," Max admitted as he sat down on his bed.

"What kind of trouble do you think they go through to make us such dishes?" Nate said, using guilt to bring Max back to reality.

"She said they had us covered," Max said as if arguing. "And when I asked her what they ate, she told me they ate the same."

"That's not our food," Nate said bluntly. "That's not *Servant's* food, to be precise."

"Don't they store their food in one pantry?" Max said, remembering when he had to clean it day after day, sorting and resorting the jars and bags that filled the room. A few moments after his question, Max realized he had gotten used to it. The lavish pantry and fridge filled with every type of food imaginable, some of which he had never known existed. Caleb might've known some of them, but there were a few special ones that looked like they belonged to the Elite and the Elite alone, particularly some cheeses that caught Max's eye.

"You thought..." Nate pointed at Max as he spoke, and then he burst out laughing and slapping his thigh. "You thought you ate from the same food as Elites? You're a Servant!"

"It wasn't smart," Max said coldly. "But it's not that funny either. I didn't see any other storage room for food."

"Wait a minute!" Nate stopped immediately, the room going silent after him. "That means you never saw the other pantry, meaning you never cleaned it."

"Yeah," Max nodded as he scratched his chin. "So?"

"When was the first-floor kitchen your duty last?"

"Before Anna went back."

"And you told me you heard shouting a while ago?" Nate said, widening his eyes as he stared at Max.

"No," Max denied reality as if it were going to change anything. "There's no way he left a room unchecked for so long. We're supposed to be cleaning every day."

"Unless it's the Servants'" Nate said gravely.

"I did this," Max said to himself. "It was my fault. Why didn't she mention it? We talked, right?" As Max drowned in guilt with Nate watching, a ringing sound came from the quarters' door, and it opened.

"That's both of us, come on," Nate said as he got up.

*****

"The winter trip has been delayed," Thorn announced coldly to his line of Servants. "That means you won't be changing duties until I say so."

The line, as usual, gave no audible reaction, but Anna's face turned into fear. Her once serene countenance contorted. Her heart skipped a beat, almost forcing her to fall over. Wide-eyed and mesmerized, her gaze fixated on the ground, hiding whatever she could. Her brows rose sharply as her mouth froze in suspended breath. The emotional turmoil swirling emanated from her. Victoria, standing by her, subtly held her up while Hannah, from the other side, stopped her from falling forward. Max and Nate noticed immediately but kept their gazes away while Thorn spouted what neither cared to hear.

"Am I clear?" An enraged call shook the five Servants.

"Yes, sir," Max invoked the usual mannerisms he put on when dealing with Thorn, but, for some reason, they were extra hard this time. Something inside Max told him he shouldn't take it and answer politely. Anna could have been really hurt by the shock, and his only reply was, 'Yes, sir.'

"Actually, no," Nate said quietly. The other four immediately turned to him, checking if they heard correctly.

"What's that?" Thorn said, spitting on Nate as he spoke. Nate looked him in the eye as he wiped his face with the back of his hand.

"I said no," Nate said, his voice loud and clear.

"Too bad, Nate," Thorn clenched his jaw as his nostrils flared with anger. "You've been a good one so far. Why?" Then, Thorn raised his hand and grabbed Nate by the shoulder. Before Nate could react, he was on the ground after receiving a hit in the neck.

"Who are you to defy me?!" Thorn screamed at Nate as he lay on the floor.

"A Servant," Max said. Thorn turned to find Max's foot hitting him clean in the jaw and pushing him away. As Thorn balanced himself, Max helped Nate up.

"You dare..." Thorn muttered as his hand went into his jacket to pull out a knife. Small yet menacing, perfectly fitting in the palm of his hand. The blade, though compact, gleamed with a malevolent glint. Its razor-sharp edge showcased a sinister precision, reflecting the intensity of the mansion entrance's lighting. A gasp came out from the women Servants as they backed away, almost dragging Anna with them.

"What do we do now?" Max whispered, frozen in place as Thorn approached with the knife.

"You defend yourself, duh!" Nate whispered back aggressively as he took Max's side.

"How are we going to do this?" Max said as he put his hands up in front of his face.

"Don't let the knife touch you," Nate said.

"I'd love to see you try," Thorn said viciously as he thrust the knife at Max, for Nate to catch his arm mid-swing. Max instinctively kicked Thorn in the stomach. The forceful strike drove the air from his lungs in a gasp of agony, and time seemed to slow down. As Max pulled his leg back for another shot, his eyes locked with Thorn, freezing him in place.

"You runts..." Thorn said between gasps, his anger at its height, nostrils flaring and eyes wide.

"We are runts," Max confirmed as he let loose another kick, landing it in the same place as the last. The sheer force of the hit shook Thorn's whole body and loosened his grip on the knife a little.

"CUT IT OUT!" Thorn threw his left fist forward, landing on Max's chest and driving him away. Nate immediately twisted the arm he held, dropping the knife to the floor. Thorn screamed in pain as he bent over, following his shoulder as it twisted. Nate held the arm as tight as he could, struggling to stay balanced.

"Max!" Nate called without looking away. Max answered in a second and punched Thorn in the stomach, letting out a burst of saliva. Thorn fought back, hitting Nate with his other arm. Nate's grip loosened for a split second, which was enough. Thorn pulled his arm away and lunged at the knife on the ground. Max followed, jumping at the knife.

*****

Hurried footsteps rushed down the stairs. Mrs. Thorn came upon a scene of her husband panting with no suit jacket, a torn button-up, and sweat covering his face. The women Servants stood by as Max and Nate stood in front of Thorn, one to his right and one to his left. Thorn's small knife lay on the ground in the middle exactly between the three. Tension stretched the air thin as the

three men eyed each other, the Servants awaiting the master to make a move. Nate's neck bled lightly, leaving a trail of red running down his suit.

"What is this all about?" Thorn said, keeping his distance and trying to catch his breath. A foulness permeated all of Thorn, voice, clothes, and countenance. His strength and authority had been challenged by his oldest Servant, nonetheless.

"What do you want?" Max retorted. "Why do you treat us like this?"

"You are a Servant," Thorn announced with disgust. "You have no right to question me. You are to serve."

"Why do we have to serve *you*?" Max taunted, his voice much louder than he intended.

"Because I am your master," Thorn's pride didn't fade one bit. "I am an Elite."

"You think that gives you the right to treat us like this?!!" Max screamed in anger as he rushed at Thorn. Thorn put his hand up to stop Max, but a knee met his stomach before he could react, and he fell forward. "You have women that serve you! At least treat *them* right! What did they ever do to you?!"

"Understand, you animal," Thorn said defiantly, although robbed of his menacing appearance by holding his stomach. "You are below me! I am better! I am Elite!"

"How's it helping you, now?" Max screamed into Thorn's ear.

"Max," Victoria's voice appeared out of nowhere, turning all eyes to her. Her eyes were teary, her voice strained, and fear decorating her face. "That's enough, please stop."

"Listen to your senior, rat," Thorn said as he struggled to straighten himself. "She knows what happens to those who defy me."

"Those who defy..." Max repeated as the words echoed in his mind.

Does that mean someone's done it before? Max's mind fished out the conclusion.

Or am I jumping? Max argued. *What does that mean, though?*

"Ask her," Thorn demanded. "Ask her what happened the last time a Servant tried to disobey me." Max's heart started racing. He looked between Victoria and Thorn for a while, doubting his own mind.

"Max, just stop," Victoria pleaded.

"What happened?" Max said, clenching his jaw. An intensity he'd never felt before took over Max's eyes as he stared at Victoria as if peering at her soul. His fists rolled up, and his muscles tensed.

"Enough, Max," Anna said, raising her face from the ground, shock and fear permeating her more than ever before.

"What happened?" Max repeated with more intensity, veins around his face and neck.

"An obnoxious runt like you tried their luck with me years before," Thorn said, visibly delighted by Victoria's fear and Max's anger.

"Shut up!" Nate bellowed as he charged at Thorn. But Thorn caught his neck and held him still.

"That runt was an ambitious little boy just like you," Thorn went on, barely holding Nate in place. "He was a good Servant at first, but after a while, he thought he was worth something, and he asked for more."

"More what?" Max's voice shook the entire room, frightening Mrs. Thorn despite her distance.

"More food, of course," Thorn said, his eyes turning more menacing than before as he stared Max down. Then, Nate hooked his leg around Thorn's angle and kicked back, dropping them both to the floor. When on the ground, Nate scurried out of Thorn's hold and hurried to his food.

"What else?" Max appeared out of nowhere, holding Thorn down. Max held him down with his entire weight, hoping it would make up for the size difference. "Talk!"

"Stop it already. You won't gain anything," Nate said, putting his hand on Max's shoulder. Nate's voice was filled with sorrow, which Max rarely saw. His entire expression was unfamiliar, especially with the blood. Max's emotions swayed left and right as his heart raced. Anger and guilt wrestled inside him, one telling him to back off and one telling him to keep going, and a third voice, lower than the rest, spoke once inside him.

You're already here. Max realized he had already gone too far. There was no going back. He, a mere Servant, had not only defied an Elite, but fought him. Touching an Elite, even if peacefully, normally meant trouble to anyone less than Elite. For a brief moment, amidst his emotional roller coaster, Max realized he had directly defied the system. A picture of Ashe flashed through his mind.

"Talk," Max turned away from Nate and focused his vision solely on Thorn. "I killed him."

At that moment, Max went blind, and his arm went loose, beating away at Thorn.

12

BLUEPRINTS OF REBELLION

"**Y**ou haven't thought of a name yet?!" Eric bellowed.

"No," Caleb grimaced, widening his eyes.

"Let's just get things together for now, we're not registering it today anyway," Dave said putting a hand on Caleb's shoulder and another on Eric's.

"How many people do we have?" Eric rushed into it.

"About sixteen, including us, if I remember correctly," Caleb said.

"Names?" Dave said, prompting a throaty chuckle from Eric.

"The most important ones," Dave said annoyedly. A knock on the door interrupted the conversation.

"Who is it?" Dave said as he stood behind the door.

"It's Alan," a familiar voice answered from outside.

"Come in," Dave said enthusiastically as he opened the door. Alan, the boy who had been asking Smith too many questions during the Depths tour, stood at the door, almost blocking the entire doorway, with two others behind him. The two looked suspiciously older than most of those Caleb, Eric, and Dave had seen before. One of them had a full beard and mustache even.

"New recruits," Alan said, not trying to hide his excitement.

"Pleasure to meet you," Dave gestured for Alan to move aside.

"Pleasure's ours," the bearded one firmly met Dave's handshake. His friend followed.

"What do we have to do?" the two said in one voice.

"Sorry to ask, what year are you?" Eric's head appeared over Dave's shoulder.

"Second, why?"

"You're our first second-year recruits, then," a warm smile came onto Eric's face. "It's an honor."

"You know we're not really a student activity, right?" Caleb whispered, his head appearing over Dave's other shoulder.

"Alan made that pretty clear," the bearded one laughed.

"Alright," Dave said commandingly, trying to get back the attention from the two standing behind him. "We still haven't registered ourselves yet. That's tomorrow. So, for now, lay low until you get any news."

"They're second years," Caleb looked at Dave. "They can help us with management."

"How do you know that?" the two second years raised an eyebrow each.

"Some guy I was recruiting earlier today," Caleb said.

"We can, actually," the bearded guy said humbly, feeling a lot older than he was. "That's part of why we came to you directly."

"You're doing some HR work, huh?" Eric said teasingly, looking at Alan.

"I do what I can," Alan dismissed the humor quietly.

"We need to know who we have, so we called a meeting after registration tomorrow," Dave explained. "7:30 at night, make sure you're there since everyone else's going to be there. We need to know each other, first of all, and decide on an MO since exams are a few days away."

"By the way, is that escape thing for real?" The other second-year asked.

"Yeah, why?" Caleb said as plainly as can be.

"Isn't that kinda big?" The same guy whispered. Caleb scanned his eyes.

"We'll discuss it tomorrow," Caleb smiled confidently as he lightly slapped the guy's shoulder.

"Pleasure to meet you, guys," Eric offered his hand, and both took it. Dave and Caleb followed before the two left.

"Nice work, man," Dave looked at Alan.

"Thanks," Alan smiled quietly.

"We're at eighteen now. That's good," Dave said reassuringly. "You go get some rest because tomorrow's a big day."

"Alright, see ya."

*****

Later that night, Caleb lay on his bed, staring at the ceiling. It had been almost a week since the Depths tour, and Eric and Dave had gone to their rooms. As Caleb lay down, his entire first semester as a Power Engineer To-Be flashed through his mind. Many lectures, many classes, and a lot of studying, yet he felt like he had learned nothing. His disgust toward the system played part, but he knew too well how much he turned away from it. The idea of striving to become one of the higher members of society was repulsive enough on its own. The idea, which had come up a while after Dave's hacking spree had started, surprised the trio.

We were that delusional, huh? Caleb thought as his head rested on his interlocked fingers. *Lifeline of a nation. More like the death of a nation.*

The prospect of escape scared him, as usual, as thoughts of backing out kept eating away at his confidence. To Caleb's logical thinking, the entire plan seemed like a hoax. Running out on his parents' dream, a prestigious job as a Verdantian engineer, and a somewhat guaranteed future.

I might even have married that Sophie girl, too. Caleb thought laughingly.

His mind calculated thousands of possible scenarios of the outcome of his little student activity gimmick. It sounded silly, like it always did. Less than twenty engineering students run away, too stressed to continue studying. What would his parents think? Then, the light bulb came on.

The parents! Caleb's eyes widened as his mind started racing through calculations. *The parents contact their children via video. No more of that in the second semester. There are excuses for that, but when the end of the year comes, we can't go back home. We're going to be wanted. I have to say that at the meeting. We're not just giving up on engineering. We're giving up on most of everything.*

As thoughts raced through Caleb's mind, disappointment filled his heart. He knew most of the parents wouldn't understand the cause, and some would even be against it. He knew his parents, Sam and Alma, would be shocked at the least. Their son has become a criminal, trying to tear apart the fabric of society itself. Fear mixed with disappointment in his mind.

*****

"How've you been?" Ashe smiled as he saw Caleb approaching through the thick shrubbery at the edge of the woods.

"Good," Caleb said, smiling weakly. "Where's Max?"

"Couldn't find him today," Ashe said, putting both legs on his pedals.

"Where're we going today?" Caleb was visibly sad, not even trying to hide his emotions.

"We don't have to ride today," Ashe said as he scanned Caleb's face. "We can just sit by the river if you want to."

"Sure," Caleb agreed, his face lighting up a little.

"Here," Ashe leaned his bike on the embankment by the river, and he plopped down on the grass, only a few inches from the water. Caleb did the same.

"What's up?" Ashe's light tone comforted Caleb.

"Stuff at home," Caleb said dismissively.

"What is it?" Ashe said, maintaining his light tone. He knew Caleb was upset but knew it wouldn't work to tell Caleb to just talk.

"You're Worker, right?" Caleb said, trying to sound as respectful as he could.

"Uhuh," Ashe nodded as he wrapped his arms around his knees.

"Are you..." Caleb said, but stopped in conscience of the consequences. "Your dad's in construction, right?"

"Yeah."

"How...is it?" Caleb struggled to form the right words, scared he might choose the wrong ones.

"How's what?" Ashe said with a chuckle. Caleb chuckled back.

"Like...life, bills," Caleb tried generalizing, hoping Ashe would get it.

"We get by, I guess," Ashe said, eyeing Caleb. "A little harder than you do, though."

"I know, but..." Caleb said, recalling the heated conversation he and Ashe had about taxes a few months before. "Does he know about our...talks?"

"He gets worried a lot," Ashe admitted after a pause. Caleb pondered the response.

Worried? So, he knows?

"Who's his boss at work?" Caleb said.

"He doesn't know," Ashe said, surprised by the question. "And neither do I, but we know he's tough to please."

"A lot of threats?"

"Entirely too many," Ashe said, airing out a little. "He's Professional, obviously,"

"Maybe that's why he's afraid," Caleb said, looking up from the ground at Ashe.

"I don't know," Ashe said quickly. "I just don't think one Professional idiot is worth all the worry. No offense,"

"I agree, actually," Caleb said quietly.

"Odd one coming out of you," Ashe teased.

"Seriously." Caleb nudged Ashe's shoulder.

"What is it then?" Ashe said, pressing Caleb to get to the point.

"Mom and Dad are kinda..." Caleb started. Immediately, a fire of conflict grew in Caleb's heart. His parents meant the world to him, usually more, yet they were mostly in favor of the system. They enjoyed the luxuries of their Stratification and often looked down upon other Stratifications. His father, Sam, was an architect, and his mother, Alma, was a surgeon. They were among the well-knowns of the Suburbs, Caleb's hometown, and they were more than kind to Caleb, raising him to be a man he was proud to be. Caleb felt indebted to them for life for all they did, and he knew how they would reject his views. "Professional."

"Don't tell them now, then," Ashe understood immediately, reading the emotions in Caleb's tone.

"For how long?" Caleb said pleadingly. "I've known you for like three years already."

"Alright, it's only three more before we're on our way," Ashe smiled.

"You want me to wait until the Crowning?!" Caleb said, shocked.

"Why not?"

"I'm already starting to look suspicious."

"Wait," Ashe stopped, hoping his doubt wasn't in place. "Do they know I exist?"

"Nope."

"Why?!" Ashe said, his voice thinning. "Just tell them I'm a friend from school who lives on the other side of town."

"How genius," Caleb mocked. "Mom works on the other side of town and knows everyone over there pretty much."

"Explaining won't do anything, will it?" Ashe tried.

"I don't think so," Caleb said disappointedly.

"Bit by bit?" Ashe said.

"It's going to take way too long," Caleb whined. "Maybe until the Crowning."

"So, what are you doing now?" Ashe said after a pause, looking at Caleb with narrow eyes.

"I'm cycling to stay in shape."

*****

"Are you ready?" Eric put his hands on Caleb's shoulders.

"Yes, speech, look into their eyes, don't lose the crowd," Caleb repeated.

"Don't look too long, though," Dave urged.

"Alright," Caleb nodded, feeling his own heart beat against his chest. "How many are in there, again?"

"Eighteen," Dave said. "Remember, we only have one hour before the hall's taken for the next lecture."

"Why don't we tell the professor?" Caleb said out of nowhere.

"Dude, what are you talking about?" Eric said forcefully, as if pushing the logic into Caleb's brain. "You went 'calculator' for a few minutes, and you're trembling thinking about talking to students alone. These teachers are still Professionals, old-fashioned too. You don't want to cross the wrong one, or we're all toast."

"Right," Caleb remembered he had thought to himself the same thing a few minutes before during his 'calculator' zone-out.

"Alright, buddy," Dave pat Caleb on the shoulder.

Then, Caleb walked onto a small stage, enough for five to stand freely, at the end of one of the Training Grounds' smaller halls. Eighteen engineering trainees of different faculties sat in front of the stage, as attentive as they were in their classes. The peering eyes terrified Caleb, and his own dived to the ground immediately as he walked up at the slowest pace he ever walked. He silently laughed at and envied his own bravery during the Depths tour when he challenged Smith out loud with everyone watching.

"Go, Caleb!" Dave cheered from behind, purposefully silly.

"WOO!" Alan cheered from among the audience. Two more slowly followed, and a few more until everyone was cheering for him to talk.

Caleb took a deep breath, and he looked up at the excited crowd, "Hi."

"Hi," the crowd answered, sounding like a roar to Caleb.

"How're you guys doing..."

"Get to it, everyone's doing good!" Eric called, forcing a laugh out of everyone, including Caleb.

"Alright," Caleb breathed as he spoke. "Let me tell you about our new student activity, Simple."

13

The Big Day

"I've had this kind of dream twice," Ashe said, leaning away from his seat as he spoke. "The common part is they were both vivid, like I was really in there, feeling the weather even."

Nolan and Aaron looked on with wide eyes, confused by the stories of a giant and a little man. Nolan's face showed mostly confusion, while Aaron's showed a mixture of confusion and fear. Ashe and Hunter looked at them expectingly, waiting for a helpful response.

"I don't really know, honestly," Aaron said first. "I've never had dreams like this before."

"This vivid or this weird?" Ashe said.

"Neither," Aaron said helplessly. "I don't have the slightest clue."

"Yeah, me neither," Nolan said confidently as he leaned back into his chair, which ached underneath his weight. "You probably came to the wrong people if you ask me. Sorry, Aaron." Aaron chuckled.

"We don't have an option, really," Ashe sighed.

"I think you shouldn't worry about it, though, Ashe," Aaron looked him in the eyes. "They were both dreams after all, maybe your subconscious is getting a little agitated by the new environment, that's all."

"New environment?"

"You know, the Hollows and all."

"Why two months apart?" Ashe challenged, prompting an awkward silence.

"They're just dreams, man," Aaron said as he scratched his head. "I know that's the last thing you wanna hear, but it's the only thing I'm getting. Sorry."

"Same here," Nolan said. "Sorry, man."

"How about we think effectively?" Hunter said brightly. "Last time, we talked about it, and we moved on, and things went well, right?"

"Yeah?" Ashe said, already concluding where Hunter was going.

"Just keep going," Hunter said encouragingly. "You're strong enough, after all." During the roughness of the past few months, Ashe had forgotten about Hunter's overwhelming positivity. The positivity which helped him accept being an Outcast in the first place.

"What I'm trying to say is this," Ashe said, his tone a lot lighter than before. "It doesn't feel like some other bad dream that goes away. I feel like it haunts me, Giant's eyes from this time especially. I think it's more than a frightening or vivid dream. I feel like it tried to...connect with me." The other three looked at Ashe, trying to find a response that would be satisfying.

"Anyways," Ashe said in an announcing manner. "Sorry I troubled you guys with this. Let's get back to work."

*****

"Has anyone come for us?" A hostage with short blond hair said a few days after Ashe's second dream. The man's face showed despair, disappointment, and a feeling of being cheated. From what Ashe and Hunter had learned earlier, the guards' training involved brainwashing them into believing they were the backbone of order on the planet and an essential key in the thriving of humanity, and that they were the government's most valuable asset. However, the government forces that did come to the Hollows never asked about their fallen comrades.

"No," Ashe said coldly. He understood the guard's pain and how much he had been let down, and he wrestled with himself not to use that pain for manipulation. After all, the man was in a vulnerable position, and his feelings were pointed in the right direction. All he needed was an exciting speech and a few cheers to have a change of mind, but Ashe wanted him to come to it on his own, despite the longer time it would take.

"Can I say something?" The guard said. The blond one had been polite for a while, unlike his teammates, which earned him Ashe and Hunter's liking.

"Sure," Hunter said, his positivity as infectious as usual.

"I quit," the man said bluntly as sweat dripped down his face.

"Quit what?" Ashe raised an eyebrow and crossed his arms.

"Whatever this is," he gestured at his worn-out uniform with his chin. Ashe beamed immediately, only to be blocked from the hostages' sight by a swift Hunter.

"How do we know this isn't a trick?" Hunter said, his positivity not waning, but his tone turning suspicious.

"I can't thank you enough for what you've done," the man's emotions exploded. "You've been treating us better than we've ever been treated. Even though you don't have much to work with, you've given us the best you could. From the food to the treatment to washing our uniforms." Then, he looked up, looking Hunter in the eye. "I want to join you."

Ashe and Hunter's faces immediately flipped. Wide eyes, parted lips, and frozen expressions. Hunter slowly turned to Ashe, gesturing for discussion.

"Alright, tiger," Ashe said, turning on his speech charisma, which he used when with crowds and when talking to many people.

"I'll do anything to prove my intentions," the man said quickly, inadvertently interrupting Ashe.

"Wait a second," Hunter said, gesturing to Ashe with his hand, then turning to the man. "Are you joining to repay us? And what's your name, by the way?"

"My name's Alex, and that's actually why I'm quitting," he said gravely. "I can't stand the situation you guys are in. I couldn't bear being held here for more than a few weeks, but you've been here for years. You were probably even worse before your farming stuff came around. I would like to thank whoever did that, too. Personally."

"You just did," Hunter said proudly, and he stepped aside, letting Ashe into the spotlight.

"You did all of this?" The three hostages said in one voice. Alex's comrades seemed like they had just woken up.

"Not exactly," Ashe said humbly.

"Dude!" Hunter slapped Ashe's shoulder.

"Gotta admit I'm impressed," the man in the middle said, breaking his long silence. "You've been lying to us, telling us you'd let us go if we gave you information, yet here we are, and now you've managed to turn one of us." The disgusted face reappeared.

"You're a stubborn one, aren't you?" Hunter's positivity immediately went away. A slightly angry look took over his face. "In the end, you're still a hostage. You don't need to know much more than that you're being kept alive. You already get the best food that we have to give, and you have a pretty good reason why you're still a hostage. So shut up if you're not going to say anything good."

"Couldn't blame you," the hostage, a red-haired youngster, spoke with an enraging voice. "This's all you can manage, anyways, Outcast." Hunter knew to keep his cool, having learned from his past experiences, with this guard in particular.

"An Outcast kid turned you into a hostage, so," Ashe said threateningly. The man turned away after raising a disgusted upper lip.

"A fluke," he spat.

"Outcasts have kept you here for over two months," Ashe raised a challenging eyebrow, maintaining his cool.

"Whatever."

"Alright, what now?" Hunter turned to Ashe, lowering his voice.

"I was going to ask *you* that," Ashe shot back.

"Should we separate him from them, then?" Hunter suggested.

"Sounds good," Ashe nodded.

"Alright, Alex," Hunter approached Alex, fishing in his pocket. *He's probably too weak to fight, anyways.*

"Thank you," Alex said sincerely as he got off the ground, shaking his hands, which had been tied to the wall above his head.

"Traitor!" The third one screamed suddenly, startling everyone.

"You're alive, huh?" Ashe muttered annoyedly.

"We'll come back to you two later," Ashe said as Hunter led Alex to the stairs.

"I'm terribly sorry for what they're doing. It's just the training and-" Alex said in the school building's main hallway.

"Don't worry about it," Hunter smiled, turning his positivity back on. "It's not your fault."

"What can I do to help? Whatever you need."

Ashe and Hunter exchanged looks as if going through the list. Food, money, manpower, better shelter, training. Training. They needed to learn how to fight. Ashe's eyes widened, remembering when they told him they had gone through extensive combat training. Alex was young, and his whole team was beaten by some Outcasts, some of whom were children, but there was still a chance he could teach the absolute basics. A particular few residents, who had the raw power but not the technique, of the Hollows flashed into Ashe's mind. These people could become the Hollows' defending force. Weaponry was, of course, a different issue.

"Can you teach us how to fight?" Ashe said. Alex's eyes went to the ground.

"I'd be too embarrassed since-" Alex said with a hushed voice. "What Ron, red hair upstairs, was saying is actually true."

"What do you mean?"

"Your beating us was a fluke," Alex said, looking around as he spoke. "We were instructed not to kill you. Our training is as rigorous as he described it. Guards in other sectors don't usually go easy."

"I can confirm *that*," Ashe said laughingly, recalling how he had tried to talk back to a guard back at his home, only to go back home with a bloody face after his father saved him.

"Why, though?" Hunter said curiously, wanting to confirm a doubt inside.

"They don't tell us," Alex said coldly. "My guess is they're afraid of situations like this." Hunter smiled at Ashe.

"Let's show them what they're afraid of, then," Ashe said excitedly.

"Ok, what can you teach us?" Hunter said.
******

For the following month, the Hollows started preparing for the meeting with the president like it was a few hours away. From Ashe's ambassador training to the farming of the yards of the buildings to Alex's combat training, the city united upon one spirit and one purpose, that of proving their power and demonstrating they weren't kneeling to a government official just because the system told them to. Guards reappeared here and there across town, inspiring some whispers and airs of suspicion as the citizens' treatment of the guards turned from their old usual of casually passing by to showing their disgust of the guards.

The hostage situation going on in the school building was already a secret to all of the Hollows, except for a trusted few, who included Aaron and Nolan. Alex's turning was hidden from most of the trusted few, and his training sessions were exclusive to Ashe and Hunter and the strongest people Ashe knew in the Hollows: the farming teacher, the four electrician brothers, and Nolan. The training sessions were held on the school building's first floor six days a week, out of the sight of both the guards roaming around and the citizens of the Hollows.

"May I ask for something?" Alex said to Ashe after a month of training sessions.

"Sure," Ashe said, wiping his sweat.

"Can I learn how to farm?" Alex said, holding his hands in front of his chest. For a split second, the contrast between the vicious instructor and the kind Alex confused Ashe.

"You know your whole situation is under wraps," Ashe explained. "The only ones who know about your turning are the seven of us and Aaron, and the only ones who know that we have hostages in the first place are two more people." Ashe saw sadness on Alex's face. "But, we can try and sneak you out of here."

"I need to blend in, right?" Alex said brightly. "This uniform doesn't look like an Outcast, though." The sadness came back to Alex's face.

"Don't worry, we'll manage that," Ashe smiled reassuringly.

"I can give you money to buy them for me, if you need it."

Ashe immediately laughed, "You think we buy clothes?" Alex's neck moved back in confusion.

"I'll let Hunter manage that for you," Ashe pat Alex on the shoulder. "But, why do you want to learn it, though? Don't you already have enough on your mind?" Ashe's mind went to the life Alex must have led behind him. He looked too young to be married, but he must have had parents. Where were they?

"I want to become one of you," Alex said with a proud smile. "I want to become an Outcast." Ashe's eyes teared up.

"How did you become a guard in the first place?" Ashe said, trying to take the attention from himself.

"Judging from your reaction to the training stories, you probably wouldn't want to know that."

14

THE OUTSIDE WORLD

"Please stop!" Mrs. Thorn's voice bellowed through the hall. Yet, Max had lost most sense of consciousness.

"MAX!" Nate screamed into his ear as he pulled him off Thorn's body. "MAX! WAKE UP!" Nate wrapped himself around Max, hugging his arms into his sides and making him completely still.

Mrs. Thorn ran down the stairs, rushing through the women Servants and sitting down on the floor next to her bloody husband. Screams, cries, wails, her voices held the same agony. The women Servants watched in a mixture of horror and shock, barely recognizing their master in his pool of blood. The body made no sound for the longest time, which made Mrs. Thorn's screams even worse until he choked. Blood came streaming out of his mouth. All the hatred, prejudice, and mistreatment built up inside Max exploded at that moment.

"Let me go!" Max said as he tried wiggling out of Nate's hold.

"Calm down, Max," Nate said into his ear. "He's almost dead. You've done enough."

"He killed! He has to die!" Max's rage emanated from his body.

"That won't do any good if you do it," Nate said with the calmest tone he could muster. "We can go now. It's over."

"Please, Max," Anna appeared in his sight. "It won't do any good to hurt him anymore. You've done enough." Max's grunts slowed down steadily.

"But...he..." Max's breathing got rapidly slower.

"Please, Max, let's just get out of here," Victoria appeared beside Anna, and slowly, Max started to regain consciousness, and Nate loosened his hold bit by bit.

"You're all going to pay for this!" Mrs. Thorn screamed at the Servants as she held the knife. "You're all going to die in a hole!"

"His phone, now!" Nate called to Anna. Anna sprinted at the man's body, dodging his wife, and she started searching his pockets.

"You don't!" Mrs. Thorn turned to the nurse, raising her knife only for Victoria to slap it away.

"Give up, or you'll end up like him," Victoria whispered to Mrs. Thorn in a menacing voice.

"You can't do this," Mrs. Thorn said, her breathing speeding up rapidly. "We are the Elite. You are Servants. You can't defy us. You can't win. You won't."

"One more word," Victoria's menacing voice, while low, froze the woman before her. Mrs. Thorn looked up at her Servant in fear.

"You're.... going.... to.... pay," the hyperventilation signs reached their peak as Mrs. Thorn held her chest.

"Hannah," Victoria commanded. Hannah swiftly appeared at Mrs. Thorn's side, catching her before she fell.

The world seemed to collapse from every direction. The Elite had fallen, and the Servants held the mansion. The Thorn family's children were not expected to come home for a long time, yet tension spiked. As Nate and Max stood up, their new reality dawned upon them.

*****

"What do we do now?" Max said, cleaning blood off his hands.

"What *can* we do?" Anna answered, pointing to the tied-up woman in fancy clothes and her unconscious husband lying on the ground beside her, tended by Hannah.

"We can't stay here for long," Victoria noted.

"How long is long?" Nate said.

"Three or four days, probably," Victoria said.

"How do you know?" Max and Anna said in one voice.

"She's the only one who's been outside since we came here," Nate said.

"You've been outside?" Max and Anna spoke in unison again.

"A few times, yes," Victoria said.

"How many is a few?" Anna said, crossing her arms.

"Once every two months. On and off."

"What for?" Max said.

"To get things they told me to," Victoria said.

"How did we not know?" Anna said in shock as she tried to hide her jealousy.

"You were always busy," Victoria said weakly. "Or asleep."

"You knew about this?" Max turned to Nate, who shied away.

"It's not his fault," Victoria said defensively.

"It's his fault he didn't say anything," Max said, prompting Nate to nod in shame.

"How long have you guys been here?" Anna said, looking between Nate and Victoria.

"Twenty-two years," Nate said.

Twenty-one." Victoria followed.

Twenty-two?!" Disbelief was splashed onto Anna's face, changing her whole countenance.

"Since Crowning, right?" Max's analytical engine threw a question out of nowhere.

"Yes," Victoria and Nate nodded. Guilt and shame immediately consumed Max.

I haven't been here for seven months, and I did that. He looked over at Thorn's body as Hannah tied it to the wall. *Twenty-two years? What have these two been through? Why did they stay silent? Why didn't they do anything? Is this what a Servant is?*

"Max, are you ok?" Nate said knowingly.

"Yeah," Max said quietly as he briefly returned to reality before drowning back into his thoughts.

"What are we supposed to do now?" Anna said with a humble look on her face.

THE ASHE WALKER CHRONICLES

"We can't tie her up like that and leave," Nate stated. "She'll probably starve."

"And I thought it was a good thing they didn't get any visitors," Anna said, tapping her chin with her forefinger. "We can't call them an ambulance or guards either."

"We're gonna have to stay until he's in good shape, too," Vicotria gestured at Thorn.

"Define good shape," Anna said.

"Can eat and drink on his own," Victoria said cheekily. "Walking isn't that urgent."

"We have to fathom the size of what we did," Nate said, staring nowhere in particular. "Whenever these two are able to communicate with the outside world, things are getting heated."

"Guards are going to search for us, you mean?" Anna said, sounding almost innocent.

"Oh no," Victoria said. "Guards are going to more or less plague this entire city."

"Why?" Anna shook her head.

"Servant and Elite," Nate said, thinking it would be enough of an explanation.

"Because he's in such bad shape?"

"Your parents were farmers, right, Anna?" Victoria said.

"Yes," Anna nodded.

"So, Workers," Victoria said. "Their district head was an Elite, right?" Anna nodded. "What happened when your father made a mistake or did something he wasn't supposed to?" Anna stayed silent for a while as if recalling her entire childhood. Then, her eyebrows went up.

"That was only for a mistake," Victoria said. "Compare that to what we did."

"But..." Anna said, her eyes still wide.

"You should've known what you were getting yourself into," Nate said. "Whether Max had exploded like he did or if we had escaped peacefully during their winter trip, the result would've probably been the same. It would've just been delayed in the second case."

"Why?" was the only thing Anna could say as horror and disgust filled her face.

"What was your Crowning like?" Max said, reappearing into the conversation.

"Disappointing, I guess. I wanted to become a Professional." Anna said. "Why are you asking?"

"How were your grades in school?" Max said, focusing extra hard.

"Good, I guess. Most everything was above 90%," Anna said.

"Then, there's a lot you need to know about the system," Nate said laughingly.

"What do you mean?"

"I can explain that later," Max promised. "We need a plan right now."

"I have an idea," Nate said, hands in his pockets. "Why don't you go outside for reconnaissance, Victoria?"

"Sounds fair to me," Victoria said. "The last time I was out was a few weeks ago, anyways. There was news about something happening in an Outcast sector nearby. It was vague, though."

"You told me about that," Nate said.

"That's how you knew, huh?" Max teased.

"Please, Max, cut him some slack," Victoria said.

"Where did you hear that?" Anna said. "Where did they send you?"

"Mostly to the market or about it," Victoria said. "It's where most of the news is shared, according to my experience."

"You grew up Servant, right?" Max said.

"Yes," Victoria answered.

For a while, the four probed through ideas, checking if any would work. Max suggested calling an ambulance and escaping quickly before they came, only for the idea to be cast aside by Nate.

"You're in an Elite district. I'll leave you to imagine how fast they are here."

The merciless thought of just leaving crept around the conversation, waiting to be pushed onto the stage. However, alternatives kept coming up, seeming to only delay the inevitable suggestion, which, looking back, didn't seem very unfair. Victoria and Nate's early days also came into the conversation, which brought the merciless suggestion infinitely close to being made. Stories of starvation, sickness, and endless pain made their marks in Max and Anna's memories. As the conversation went on, Max's analytical engine tried to remember the look of the city he had only got to see briefly half a year before and to base plans on it.

"That's another issue, actually," Nate pointed out.

"We don't know enough about the outside world," Vicotria explained. "I *have* been out, but I'm not even close to knowing where to go and how to."

"There's so much out there we don't know," Max murmured to himself.

"All done," Hannah said as she approached the group.

"Nice work, Hannah," Victoria smiled at the nurse, who looked about Max's age.

"What have you decided?" She looked innocently at everyone, avoiding Max. "Are we going to the Outcast sector?"

"Our current issue is these two," Nate pointed at the Thorns.

"Oh, we don't have to worry about them," Hannah said, traces of mischief in her voice. The entire group looked at her, waiting for an answer.

"I bandaged him enough for her to take care of him for a day or two," Hannah said. "Then, she's supposed to call an ambulance. That's enough for us to get out of the city, right?"

"How do you know she won't call one right after we leave?" Victoria challenged. While not hiding that she was impressed.

"Well," Hannah half-smiled. "I threatened her we'd come back here and kill them both if she did." The entire group went silent.

"Why didn't you say so in the beginning?" Anna said laughingly. "You would've saved us a lot of time."

"Were you guys discussing a plan all this time?" Hannah barely held her laugh.

"Pretty much," Nate said coldly.

"That's one problem solved," Max said. "We still don't know where to go or how to."

"The how is simple if you or Nate can drive," Victoria said.

"I can, yes," Nate said as his eyes lit up.

"They have a car," Victoria explained. "Although it's more of a van."

"I didn't see it when I came here, though," Max said, scratching his head as he vaguely remembered the luxurious sights of the main street outside.

"Neither did I," Hannah added.

"Vehicles are parked in the back on Crowning days," Victoria said. "Or whenever the street's expected to be crowded."

"Alright, the where is our issue now," Max said, mainly to himself to sort ideas in his head.

"We can go to the market and ask there," Anna said after what felt like a prolonged silence.

"Ok, we're just gonna have to hide the car," Nate noted.

"I'll go in as if shopping," Victoria offered.

"Go get your badge then," Nate gestured toward the mansion gates.

"I'll be right back," Victoria hurried out.

"What badge?" Max said.

"Only Elites are allowed to buy from the markets here, obviously," Nate said bluntly. "But if they're too lazy to do so, they can get their Servants to do their shopping for them, and that requires identification, made by the government so we don't get creative."

"So, we have badges, too?" Max said.

"Thorn only made one for Victoria," Nate said, not trying to hide the envy in his voice.

15

A New Dawn

"To conclude, our new activity Simple is supposed to make studying easier, faster, and more fun," Caleb said, his hands going everywhere. "If you have any questions, ask away." A few hands shot up into the air.

"He didn't have a finisher," Eric said disappointedly.

"Go ahead," Caleb looked at one of the students who raised their hands, a first-year boy with short black hair and tan skin. His build was thin and tall, with a determined look on his face.

"Where is the rebellion part?"

The entire room turned to the boy, eyebrows rising and jaws dropping. Caleb froze for a moment, thinking he heard wrong but confirming what he heard by the room's reaction. An engineering student, a Professional, had just made an open remark about rebellion, and in the house of Professionals, the Verdantia Engineering Training Grounds A. Eric and Caleb both stood still, on edge. After a few tense seconds of silence, all eyes went to Caleb, waiting for him to act.

Did he just say rebellion? The thought kept echoing in Caleb's head until he realized all eyes were on him.

"Caleb!" Eric called.

"Uhm..." Caleb looked around the room, fearing what he was going to say. Then, he realized the boy in front of him had just asked about a rebellion on Professional grounds. "Did you just say rebellion?"

"Yeah," the boy nodded, his casual manner his most shocking trait. "I asked where the rebellion part is."

"I'm sorry, what is the rebellion *part* you're talking about?" Caleb put on the same smile he had on during the presentation.

"When we were told about the whole student activity thing, the guy tried to imply it, but it was too obvious," the boy smiled, a joyful humor about him. "Or did I get it wrong?"

"Does the person you're talking about happen to be this guy?" Caleb pointed at Alan, who was sitting at the front. Eric's face fell into his palm.

"Yeah!" The boy said enthusiastically after he craned his neck to check.

"Well," Caleb looked around. *There's the elephant in the room. They don't seem too surprised now, that's good. He actually made it easier, like tenfold. We can get into it right away.* Caleb snuck a look at everyone's faces to find anticipating, expecting looks and no looks of fear or outrage. "Alright, do I have to formally talk this out, guys, or can we just get into it?"

"Get into it," the crowd, including Alan, said in unison.

"Ok, you guys probably already knew or suspected this student activity is actually a cover," Caleb said, his tone turning more serious than its bright version during the presentation. "Simply put, we don't like the system, and we want to take it down. We know it's weird coming out of Professionals, but you've probably already thought the same about yourself if you're sitting here. We plan on escaping the grounds and not coming back after the exams, and we planned this student activity façade to try and find anyone who shared our views, and here we are. That's our story in a nutshell," Caleb gestured at Eric and Dave, who stood off the stage to the left. "Does anyone have any questions?"

"How is this going to work?" A boy with glowing red hair said right away. "Are you going to be the leaders, and we're going to be divided into squads or what?"

"That's a great question," Caleb smiled as he gestured for Eric and Dave to come closer. "We were thinking about having it that way before, uhm, today, but I don't think that matters anymore." Then, Caleb gestured for Eric to speak.

"The three of us became friends uniting around this purpose," Eric said, taking center stage. "We originally wanted to gather you around us as friends, with the student activity thing being a cover at first." Eric sighed with the relief of getting his sentence out correctly. His nerves felt like a roller coaster, and he immediately vowed to himself not to blame Caleb for his stage fright ever again.

"What is escape supposed to do, though?" A particularly fiery boy said. He had a muscular build, straight posture, and chestnut hair.

"What else can we do?" Eric said the first thing on his mind, fearing being silent too long in front of the crowd.

"Has any one of you taken the Networks course yet?" The boy said.

"Yes," Dave came into view with his hand in the air.

"Anyone else here?" Six of the seated students raised their hands.

"You know about the data center on the Grounds, right?" The boy said. Dave immediately beamed.

"I've taken a few peaks, why?" Dave said, resisting his pride with all his might.

"We're eight in total. If we can launch an attack on the data center at the right time, it's going to be way more problematic than a few runaways who couldn't handle the studious nature of being Professionals," the boy said.

"You hacked the data center?" One of the boys who raised his hand looked at Dave admiringly.

"Not exactly," Dave blushed. "I learned a few things on my own before I came here, and the Networks course extended that. I could only look at certain data. I could edit nothing, and there was some stuff that I couldn't see."

"What *did* you see?" The chestnut-haired boy asked.

"The most dangerous thing was power distribution records," Dave said gravely. "Worker districts get power cuts for Elite and Professional districts to have their lights and factories on 24/7. That includes Worker hospitals." Everyone went silent for a few seconds, taking in the news.

"Then, what's left for you to see are the weaponry files, I think," the chestnut-haired boy said. "Nice work getting to the distribution records, though."

"How do you know all of this?"

"I did a little peaking myself at the beginning of the year," the boy admitted.

"That sounds good, but it's not enough," Alan protested. "If you launch an attack, maybe some servers will crash, but it'll just be fixed. We need something physical alongside it. To leave a mark."

"I agree," ten attendees said in one voice.

Wow, Caleb thought. *Are they being serious?* In Caleb's mind, especially from his experience with Eric and Dave, everything so far had been talk and hopes. Now, there were people united around them and discussing actual actions they were going to take. Twenty-one students weren't many compared to the rest, but they were definitely strong enough to make a difference.

"Set something on fire?" The chestnut-haired boy said enthusiastically.

"Yeah!" Everyone cheered.

"Not too loud everyone. We're still behind enemy lines," Eric said shyly.

"Sorry," the crowd said in one loud voice.

You're engineering students, man. Eric's face fell into his palm.

"Alright, here's the plan," Caleb said.

*****

The group who attended the meeting were eighteen, including Alan. So, the member count of the student activity, Simple, was twenty-one, including Eric, Dave, and Caleb, who was appointed organizer of the activity. After the meeting, everyone went back to their usual activities under the cover of having to postpone their activities because of the exams. However, the eighteen were unofficially divided into three teams, according to the plan described by Caleb at the meeting. The first team, made up of eight students, was the hacking team, led by Dave. The second team was the management team, made up of Caleb, Eric, and the two second-year students whom Alan had brought. The third team was directly under the management team, from whom they got specific tasks.

The grand plan, devised by the entire twenty-one-man group together, was set to start on the first day of the first semester's exams, the day which happened to have all three years sitting for exams at the same time. Exams on the Training Grounds were all taken via computer labs, with each lab assigned a group of students according to their names. Caleb and Dave had the same lab for their first exam, while Eric had the following one on the higher floor. So, each team took their position, and the hacking team awaited the signal to start their attack.

"Do you smell smoke yet?" The chestnut-haired boy named Noah nudged Dave's shoulder.

"No," Dave said calmly as he looked into his phone. The two sat inside the data center, almost shivering in the room's temperature as they hid behind the towering racks of devices. "Check on the rest of the team."

"They distributed right, but it's going to be a little tough considering how wide they're spread," Noah muttered to himself.

"It's not the best technical way, but our safety still takes priority," Dave explained. "We can't all gather in one room for them to just come in and catch us." Then, a bang sounded outside.

"One," Noah counted.

"Ready," Dave demanded as his fingers started flying across his keyboard. Noah did the same. A second bang sounded outside.

"One to go," Dave said urgently as tension started rising.

"Guys, one to go," Noah said into his phone.

"On it," a faint response came back.

After the second sound, Dave and Noah started hearing footsteps outside, and their hearts came up to their throats. As they awaited the third explosion, the air seemed to leave the room, not letting them retake their breaths. Then, after about a minute of silence, wide eyes, and tense muscles, the third and loudest bang sounded, and the tension released.

"Launch!" Noah shouted into his phone as he and Dave pressed the final keys on their laptops and looked at each other.

"Should be on in three," Dave started.

"Two," Noah continued.

"One." The two said in one voice, and the sound of footsteps flooded the outside.

"Let's get out of here," Dave jumped away from his laptop as he grabbed Noah's hand to help him up. "We gotta catch the crowds before they're out of here." When the two opened the door to the data center, they came upon chaos.

Smoke rose out of three windows in three of the corner buildings around the campus, and its smell filled the air. Students, professors, and workers alike ran about the campus, each in a direction of their own. Fear consumed their faces as they were caught in a whirlwind of panic. The usual order and tranquility that graced the campus had been shattered. Amidst the turmoil, a sense of disarray prevailed. Students clutched their books and personal belongings, their hands trembling. The shrill sound of alarms pierced the air, adding to the cacophony of hurried footsteps and anxious voices. The once-familiar grey garden and fountain now resembled a maze of confusion as people desperately sought escape from the impending danger. Snippets of fragmented conversations filled the air, heightening the tension and uncertainty that gripped the atmosphere.

"Where's everyone?" Noah said as loudly as he could.

"I can't see a thing," Dave responded to what he thought he heard. Then, Noah pulled his shoulder and gestured towards the front gate, which they had come through after the Crowning.

"Let's go," Dave mouthed, and the two turned, mixing into a group of the crowd.

*****

"No more phones," Eric said, putting his hand on Caleb's shoulder.

Caleb looked up at Eric, then out his dorm room's window to find the panicking crowds running around campus. "I didn't think it would be that effective."

"Fear works with this type of crowd, usually," Eric said quietly. "Come on, everyone's probably heading for the gate now."

"Caleb! We're heading down!" Alan's voice came through Caleb's phone.

"Come on, already," Eric said, turning toward the door. Caleb nodded, and the two left the dorm room, leaving behind everything.

The plan, formulated by the entire group, was meticulously designed to take down everything at the same time. The first step was the physical one. Alan and his team were to go to certain labs in buildings and then bomb machines. The entire Grounds' focus was on the computer labs, where the exams were held, thus making the task easier. The second step of the plan was the fear factor and the first one to start. The hacking team was to send ominous messages to all the students they could every four hours, starting two days before the first exam. The third and last step was the breakdown. Cutting all the computer labs out from the servers during the exam. Finally, the group was supposed to escape the Grounds amidst the chaos. However, reality showed otherwise.

As soon as Caleb and Eric were on the campus, they went for the gates, dodging students running for their lives and those scurrying to the dorm building to get their belongings.

Way to go for a hap-hazardous plan, Caleb thought worriedly. *Hope nothing goes wrong.*

"Hey," Eric pointed at the front gates as they swung open. Caleb's eyes widened as they both stopped in their tracks, and armed guards flooded the campus.

Made in the USA
Columbia, SC
06 August 2024

39590316R00059